PLAYERS AND PAINTED STAGE

RTÉ
The 2004 Thomas Davis Lectures

PLAYERS AND PAINTED STAGE
Aspects of the Twentieth Century Theatre in Ireland

EDITED BY
CHRISTOPHER FITZ-SIMON

PLAYERS AND PAINTED STAGE
First published 2004
by New Island
2 Brookside
Dundrum Road
Dublin 14
www.newisland.ie

Copyright © 2004 RTÉ

The authors have asserted their moral rights.

ISBN 1 904301 63 0

British Library Cataloguing in Publication Data. A CIP catalogue record for this
book is available from the British Library.

Typeset by New Island
Cover design by New Island
Printed by CPD, Ebbw Vale, Wales

10 9 8 7 6 5 4 3 2 1

CONTENTS

INTRODUCTION

This series of Thomas Davis Lectures has been occasioned by the celebrations marking the centenary of the opening of the Abbey Theatre – Ireland's national theatre – on 28 December 1904. While an immense amount has been written (and said) about the Abbey Theatre over the last hundred years, it is not the purpose of these talks to evaluate further the Abbey's position either now or at any previous time: this has been very adequately done elsewhere. Rather, the contributors – distinguished theatrical practitioners, critics and academics – were asked to consider the broader scheme of the twentieth century theatre in Ireland, to identify aspects which may have been neglected or forgotten, to connect important events or movements by theme or topic rather than by personality or chronology and to delineate contexts which seem to have been ignored or glossed over by earlier commentators.

This may be a somewhat oblique, not to say dismissive, way of saluting the Abbey's achievement, but surely it hardly needs to be pointed out that the Abbey's unique contribution to the drama of the western world in the earlier part of the twentieth century continues to be the subject of international wonderment and inquiry, and that the Abbey persists in maintaining its position of pre-eminence as the chief producer of new plays in Ireland and as the chief instrument for the encouragement of young playwrights. During its centenary year, when the greater part of the programme is devoted to major productions that reassess the company's own plays of the past and acknowledge its European connections, no less than five new Irish plays are being presented on its stages.

Indeed, it would appear that almost any theatrical enterprise in Ireland during the last hundred years may be traced in some inextricable way back to the Abbey, either as a means of emulating the Abbey's accomplishment or of attempting to escape from its thrall. Hilton Edwards and Micheál MacLíammóir established the Dublin Gate Theatre in 1928 to offer the public, and also their actors, an alternative to plays which always seemed to be set in peasant cabins, provincial parlours or city tenements (quite a wide spectrum of locations, it must be said!) and to offer work of a much wider and — as it seemed at the time — more exotic provenance. More recently, with the blurring of constitutional niceties, the Gate's play selection has strayed into what would have been seen as the Abbey's territory — but then the Abbey may be said to have strayed into the Gate's. The Lyric Players Theatre in Belfast was founded in 1951 to create 'a poets' theatre', very much on the lines of the theatre which Yeats had hoped to establish in Dublin – but this enterprise produced hardly any original poetic drama and indeed comparatively few original plays of any kind, and only one that can be accounted a masterpiece. Instead, a conventional regional theatre emerged with local dramatists sharing the stage with the international classics and, in fair measure, plays taken from the Abbey's repertoire. By contrast, the Druid Theatre Company in Galway, founded in 1975, has produced several new Irish plays of significance, but has perhaps shown its greatest moments of creativity in its reinterpretation of plays which began on the Abbey stage, often providing a more vivid and confrontational *mise-en-scène* than the Abbey was able to muster. The Field Day Theatre Company, inaugurated in Derry in 1981, was seen by observers – largely overseas, it must be said – to be set to rout the Abbey entirely and become the most important force in Irish drama, its sequence of undoubted masterpieces from Brian Friel, Seamus Heaney, Thomas Kilroy and others placing the Abbey amongst the also-rans; yet this did not happen, for Field Day slowly expired from a surfeit of cultural theory and a dearth of practicality. The Abbey has, consciously or otherwise, assisted at the birth of many interesting and vibrant ensembles, and has contrived to survive them all.

There are two contextual components which seem to have been missed by almost all commentators upon the early Abbey Theatre, and without which the company would not have survived a week. The first was the existence of an extensive ready-made, sophisticated, socially diverse and inquisitive theatre-going public. The second was a highly opinionated daily and weekly press used to reviewing every imaginable production, from parish drama groups and university amateurs to visiting productions of plays from Shakespeare to Pinero, from Ibsen to Sardou, with much fervour and at great length. Until comparatively recently, the opinions expressed by most critics reflected the policy of the publications for which they wrote, supposedly coinciding with the views of the particular paper's readership.

There are, of course, dozens of fascinating subjects which we might have explored were it not for the natural constraints imposed by the form of the eight-talk series. No attempt has been made to embrace every neglected aspect of the Irish theatre during the last century, and indeed such a notion would be unthinkable. It is hoped, however, that listeners and readers will find the present selection of topics to be both enticing and provoking – qualities which, indeed, have informed our willful and iridescent theatre for over a hundred years.

Christopher Fitz-Simon

POSTER FOR AN IRISH NATIONAL COMPANY TOURING
PRODUCTION OF HUBERT O'GRADY'S *EMIGRATION*,
SEEN AT THE GRAND OPERA HOUSE, BELFAST, IN
1884. THE PLAY ACHIEVED OVER FIVE THOUSAND
PERFORMANCES, MAINLY IN BRITAIN.

Riddell Collection, Belfast Public Libraries.

CHRISTOPHER FITZ-SIMON

1904: RICHNESS AND DIVERSITY WITHOUT THE ABBEY

Few commentators over three generations have mentioned what the general public may therefore hardly be expected to know – that the Abbey Theatre came into being at an unusually prosperous period for the theatre in Ireland. Indeed, the considerable body of theatrical history and biography seems to suggest that the Abbey arrived at a time of stage famine in Ireland – which the facts do not support. It is almost as if someone in the early years of the twentieth century had decided to let the tide of scholarship wash away all evidence of *other* manifestations of theatre from our shores, leaving the Abbey sparkling on the beach like the changeling starfish that indeed it is.

A hundred years ago the Irish theatre was largely a colonial institution – yet containing a defiantly nationalistic element which lurked on certain larger stages as if in readiness to replace, at a signal moment, the bland imports from the West End. This would have to be a difficult task, for Britannia provided a much wider choice of attractions to the Irish theatre-goer than anything remotely realisable at home (and, as a matter of fact, a wider choice than anything available today). In 1904 the professional theatres in Ireland were entirely 'receiving' theatres – they did not produce their own material, which came to them *via* a number of cross-channel commercial touring circuits; even the occasional Irish dramas were a component of these circuits.

There were fine theatres in Derry, Limerick, Waterford and Wexford receiving productions for most of the year – they were known as 'No. 2 Venues' because they were not technically equipped to accommodate the most lavish London productions of, say, Gilbert & Sullivan or William Shakespeare. Other 'No. 2' venues were the Alhambra and the Empire in Belfast, the still-existing Palace in Cork and the Tivoli and Empire in Dublin – the latter survives as the Olympia. There were five 'No. 1' venues open all the year round: Belfast's Theatre Royal and Grand Opera House – the latter still with us in all its Hindu-Baroque splendour – Dublin's Theatre Royal and Gaiety and Cork's magnificent Opera House. The Gaiety is a real survivor; one senses that although it did not receive the most spectacular West End shows a hundred years ago, it was favoured by a rather more genteel clientèle. There was, as yet, no cinema; and, in Dublin, on any night, there were over 6,500 theatre seats on sale.

There was also an eccentric theatre at the intersection of Brunswick and Tara streets: the Queen's. Very much a No. 2, most of its weekly attractions were light London comedies, thrillers and melodramas with the odd week of opera or musical comedy. Many of these shows would have been snaking around London's suburban ring, from the Golders Green Hippodrome to the Metropole in Camberwell and thence perhaps to the Salford Prince-of-Wales or Merthyr Tydfil Royal – often arriving at the Dublin Queen's after fifty-two weeks or more on the road. It was also at the Queen's that, quite regularly throughout the year, *Irish* plays could be seen, mainly produced by Mr J. Kennedy Miller's Combination, but sometimes by other companies – some of them, surprisingly, based in England.

The year 1904 in Dublin saw the usual forty-six weeks of variety and eight weeks of panto in the No. 2 houses. Operas heard were *Faust, Carmen* and *The Lily of Killarney* (by the Moody Manners Company at the Royal) and *Faust, Mignon, Carmen, Rigoletto, Trovatore, The Daughter of the Regiment, Tristan & Isolde, Tannhauser, The Bohemian Girl* and *The Lily of Killarney* (all by the Carl Rosa Opera at the Gaiety) and the Elster Grimes Opera Company was heard for two weeks in *Faust* and *Maritana* (at the Queen's). It seems that every opera company always brought at least one of the components of the Irish Ring when touring in Ireland; while *The Lily of Killarney* was at the Royal during the week before Christmas, there was a perceptible nod from one house to the other as the Queen's was performing Mr Boucicault's original play of *The Colleen Bawn*. These were local quirks, not shared by Warrington or Northampton.

In the year of the opening of the Abbey Theatre, Shakespeare was seen in Dublin in the repertoire of three visiting companies: Sir Herbert Beerbohm Tree gave *Twelfth Night, The Merry Wives of Windsor* and *Julius Caesar* at the Royal in April, F.R. Benson gave *Othello, Richard II,*

Macbeth and *Hamlet* at the Gaiety in early November and this was followed only two weeks later at the same house by Sir John Martin Harvey as Hamlet, an interpretation which had caused tremendous debate in London. The country was criss-crossed by railway-travelling Shakespearians – Tree's and Benson's companies both went on to Belfast, with a space of only two weeks between them. In Cork, Edmund Tearle gave *Othello*, *Richard III*, *The Merry Wives of Windsor* and *As You Like It* at the Opera House: for which there were special supporters' trains from Mallow, Youghal, Bandon and Macroom.

As if this were not enough, there were the non-Shakespearian, non-operatic, non-vaudevillian attractions: over fifty week-long presentations in the year. It will hardly prove profitable to examine titles such as *Her One Great Sin*, *The Anarchists' Terror* or *Mysteries of the Thames*, but there was much which must impress: Sarah Bernhardt at the Gaiety in (what but?) Dumas *père*'s *La Dame aux Camélias* and Sardou's *La Sorcière*, in French, of course. Madame Bernhardt played in Dublin for a fortnight, while one week was considered sufficient for Manchester and *one night* for Belfast. Sir Henry Irving came to the Theatre Royal with a mixed bag of somewhat threadbare favourites, heavily disguised in sumptuous costumes and spectacular scenic effects – Tennyson's *Beckett*, Leopold Lewis's melodrama *The Bells* and Casimir de la Vigne's court intrigue *Louis XI*. The Compton Comedy Company brought *She Stoops to Conquer*, *The Rivals* and *The School for Scandal* to the Gaiety – there was nothing in the publicity to suggest that Dublin should have a special interest in these plays any more than Doncaster.

With such widespread uniformity of product, from Cardiff to Cork, anything even slightly different would have stood out; such was patently the case with the Irish plays presented mainly at the Queen's, though not exclusively there. In January 1904 there was a revival of J.W. Whitbread's patriotic play *Theobald Wolfe Tone* by the J. Kennedy Miller Combination. It had been written in 1898 to coincide with the centenary of the 1798 insurrection and since then had been almost continuously on the road throughout the British Isles along with Kennedy Miller's other productions. Two weeks later at the Queen's Kennedy Miller presented another revival, this time of a much older play with an Irish setting, *The Green Bushes* by John Buckstone. First produced at Covent Garden in 1845, it deals with the involvement of a young Irish landowner in the Jacobite Rebellion of 1745 and his adventures in exile in Mississippi. A bizarre, almost surreal, work, it had become established as the archetypal Hibernian drama and was constantly revived here, though the author was not Irish: but its influence on subsequent Irish playwrighting, particularly on the young Boucicault, was immense.

Returning from another tour in April 1904, Kennedy Miller revived two more Whitbread plays at the Queen's — *The Irishman* and *The Victoria Cross. The Irishman* had been premièred in London fifteen years before and subsequently presented by Kennedy Miller in his touring repertory almost annually: the London critics were impressed by the realism of its eviction scene and the nationalist press in Ireland was pleased that London realised that such things were not fanciful theatricalities. *The Victoria Cross* was quite a different matter. First given at the Queen's in 1896, it is Whitbread's only non-Irish play. The setting is the flowering lawns of the Aubrey family estate in the Home Counties and Cawnpore on the Ganges at the time of the Indian Mutiny. It has no Irish connection save the character of Andy Cregan, an Irish soldier-servant – no production was considered complete without the popular Ulster actor Frank Breen in this part. *The Victoria Cross* appeared at the Grand Opera House in Belfast early in its first tour, in the presence of Field Marshall The Rt Hon. Lord Roberts, Commander of HM Forces in Ireland. This significantly disposes of a historical myth about Whitbread and his plays – that he only wrote patriotic Irish melodramas and that his audience was entirely confined to the nationalist sector. The fact is his plays on Irish patriotic themes were performed all over the British Isles, and when he chose to set one in a different milieu members of the Viceregal circle had no difficulty in attending – in fact they were probably very glad to find an easy opportunity of lending patronage to the genuine Irish stage.

During the summer of the year in which the Abbey Theatre was to open there were revivals at the Queen's of Dion Boucicault's three most popular plays, *The Colleen Bawn*, *Arrah na Pogue* and *The Shaughran* – now thirty, forty and forty-four years old respectively. Boucicault's plays epitomise the romantic Irish comedy, with their good-humoured nationalist sentiments which could undoubtedly be emphasised to suit the mood of a particular audience on a particular night. It is unlikely that Kennedy Miller and his players – or the audiences to whom they played – were aware that a new group calling itself the 'Irish Literary Theatre' had written harshly about this type of drama, employing the word 'buffoonery'. The Kennedy Miller Combination had its own much larger clientèle to satisfy, and what was more it engaged Irish professional actors and stage crews and did not make a pretence of Irishness while hiring its talent in London. By 1904 the Literary Theatre, with its attendant poets, seers and tweedy Celtic Revivalists from Rathgar, had evolved as the 'National Theatre Society' under the presidency of William Butler Yeats and was certainly engaging some local talent – such as the brothers Frank and Willie Fay – but they were performing in church halls and their only productions in the first three-quarters of the year were of one-act plays. Next, Kennedy Miller brought back two Whitbread favourites, *Lord Edward* and *The Insurgent Chief.* The latter is a rambling piece about the Scarlet Pimpernel-like escapades of Michael Dwyer, gleaned from a book published in 1869 and brought out on the stage in Dublin and elsewhere while the commemoration fever of '98 was still in the air; it has little to do with history – which the Lord Edward Fitzgerald play more obviously has – but that was hardly the point. A well-spoken Welsh actor, Fred Lloyd, was cast as both Fitzgerald and Dwyer, but the largest part in both plays was not the nominal hero but the broth-of-a-boy man-of-the-people, played by the comedian James O'Brien. This was the same James O'Brien who only a dozen years later would employ the young Cyril Cusack in his touring company, and whom Cusack revered as a kind of mentor. In *Lord Edward* O'Brien was cast as Thady McGrath, Lord Edward's faithful factotum, and in *The Insurgent Chief* as Dwyer's henchman Hughie Byrne – the parts are quite stereotypical and it must have been left very much to the actor to supply them with individuality.

It is natural that the low critical regard in which popular plays of this kind were subsequently held was principally due to their melodramatic quality. Originally 'music drama', melodrama attracts attention by its swift-moving story and its instantaneous appeal to basic human concerns. The author does not waste time on niceties of verisimilitude or on the believability of the situations: he uses a kind of dramaturgical shorthand and it is the actors' job to create the enveloping style which will lessen the sense of improbability – in other words, the players, and indeed the scenic designers and the orchestra, paper over the authorial cracks. The style is almost invariably rhetorical – it had to be, for late nineteenth century building technology was creating larger theatres where natural speech and gesture could hardly reach the furthest recesses. The actor had to convey feelings by means of declamation and exaggerated gestures and glances.

This is not to say that all the popular plays at the time of which I'm speaking were melodramas, but most of them had some melodramatic element – from Tennyson's *Beckett* to Dumas' *La Dame aux Camelias*. (Shaksepeare adapted very well to the melodramatic style of production.) What distinguished *Irish* melodrama from its English and American counterparts was its patriotic component. The lovely (and often witty) Irish heroine was much more than a wronged Maria Marten (of *Murder in the Red Barn* fame) or Isobel (of *East Lynne*): whether peasant or gentlewoman she was an embodiment of nationhood, albeit less subtly drawn than in the work of the *aisling* poets of a hundred years before. The hero of Irish melodrama, if not determinedly choosing the road to the gallows to assuage his country's wrongs, was usually trying to create a measure of agrarian or social reform. There was a strong tendency for the central male character to be presented as a figure with whom the audience could readily identify – whether fictional like Hervy Blake in J.B. Fagan's *The Rebels* or history-inspired like Henry Joy McCracken in Whitbread's *The Ulster Hero*. The villain in Irish melodrama was quite different from the mustachio-twirling toff intent on securing the hapless maiden: he was the conniving agent of an absentee landlord or, worse, an informer against those of his countrymen who were seeking to pave the path towards liberty. Interestingly enough, the villain in these plays is hardly ever an English redcoat or justice of the peace (who may be seen to be doing their distasteful duty); he is called by an indigenous name like Rafferty or Flannigan and is therefore to be all the more hated and despised as a traitor.

In Irish melodrama, the servants and rustics who aid and support their patriotically disposed masters are, as a matter of course, aiding the cause of national liberty. These roles are generally the largest and most amusing, designed to create a lively rapport with the audience; almost always they were given to the best actors, like O'Brien and Breen and the character comedienne Monica Kelly, to whose sallies the audience rose with acclaim.

In October–November 1904 there was a kind of end-of-an-era visit to the Queen's of Hubert O'Grady's Irish National Company in *The Famine* and *The Fenian*, under the direction of Mrs O'Grady, Mr O'Grady having died in England on a recent tour. O'Grady was the author of by far the most original and the most politically and socially provocative body of Irish plays seen in the final quarter of the nineteenth century. Born in Limerick in 1841, he emigrated to Liverpool where he became involved initially in negro minstrelsy and panto, subsequently developing his own Irish sketches on the music-hall circuit. When he was thirty-five he and his wife were seen by Boucicault and immediately engaged for a tour of *The Shaughran*, opening at the Theatre Royal, Edinburgh: O'Grady played the eponymous hero, becoming, after eleven months, the earliest Shaughran to be seen on the Dublin stage — his was, by all accounts, a triumphant visit to the Theatre Royal. He then bought the rights from Boucicault, formed his own company and started writing

Irish dramas with the Boucicault tune in his head. As he progressed, he introduced a much more socially critical element, as his titles show – as well as *The Famine* and *The Fenian*, there followed *Emigration, The Eviction* and *The Priest-Hunter*. O'Grady maintained a full-time touring ensemble of upwards of fifty actors, musicians and technicians for over twenty years, appearing regularly at the No. I theatres of the chief British cities, including London. One might enquire what attraction had very specifically Irish plays for the English public: the only answer must be that they told an engaging story well, and certainly topics such as emigration or eviction were equally germane to people living in the industrial cities of the midlands – or Wales or Scotland for that matter.

In Ireland O'Grady's productions drew enormous crowds. It is extraordinary that the Castle authorities did not take repressive action, for all these plays contain highly explosive material; there are reports of an attempt to ban a production of *The Eviction* at the Queen's, but either this was successfully resisted by O'Grady or the Castle decided it was better to leave well alone. The plays were all passed as 'suitable for performance' by the Lord Chamberlain's office in London and, while the censor's remit did not technically extend to Ireland, this imprimatur was surely a fair enough certificate. It is quite clear from examining the manuscripts that the Lord Chamberlain's readers did not take their duties very strenuously, affixing the stamp of approval after a cursory inspection. Furthermore, O'Grady knew how to play the system, misleading the censor with handwritten memos such as – 'This Drama is simply a Romantic Irish Love Story and has nothing to do with Patriotic, Political or Local Evils'! Why bother, then, the censor was being advised, to read on? O'Grady submitted only the first act of *Emigration*, making it appear to be a one-act play – no doubt correctly assuming that it would be most unlikely for the bored official to follow up his reading by a visit to the Princess's Theatre, Glasgow, where it opened.

All the Irish plays given in Ireland during the first eleven months of 1904 – with the exception of the one-acters by Yeats, Cousins and Synge seen in the Molesworth Hall – were large-scale revivals. At the very end of the year, however, J.W. Whitbread gave a new piece to the Kennedy Miller Combination, *Sarsfield*, and this was premièred at the Queen's on St Stephen's Night. *Sarsfield* uses the Siege of Limerick and the Flight of the Wild Geese as the stirring backdrop to a fictional intrigue between two eminent noblewomen for the attentions of the great Irish general, but the chief character is not a member of this triangle but the rapparee of folk memory, Galloping Hogan, here portrayed as Sarsfield's trusty servant and helpmate and played (of course) by James O'Brien. This conventional but proficient piece, as expected, drew plaudits from the popular press and cheers from the public. The following night the Abbey Theatre opened for the first time with Yeats's *On Baile's Strand* and Lady Gregory's *Spreading the News*.

It looks suspiciously as if the PR-conscious Queen's had anticipated the inauguration of a potential rival theatre and had determined to damage it at birth with the double stratagem of stealing its publicity by opening the previous night and by giving the Dublin audience a new sure-fire patriotic melodrama. *Sarsfield* played its advert-ised fortnight to full houses, moving on immediately to Glasgow and other cities. The Abbey played its seven nights and then closed, in order to prepare for Synge's *The Well of the Saints*. Yet it is impossible to detect malice on the part of the Queen's Theatre – it is much more likely that its management did not even notice the arrival of the newcomer, or if they did they saw the Abbey as merely another of those idealistic enterprises that would evaporate once its socialite perpetrators moved on to other arcane activities. It is much easier to detect ineptitude on the Abbey's part in announcing their opening to coincide with such an eye-catching theatrical event as *Sarsfield*.

It would, of course, be plays like *Sarsfield* and production-companies like Kennedy Miller's and Hubert O'Grady's that would shortly evaporate. They would not be replaced by art theatres like the Abbey, which would take on a particular cultural importance of their own, but by the cinema, which could deal with the spectacle and the vivid emotions much more effectively at a high level of popular enjoyment. The Abbey and the Queen's were not therefore rivals, because they were engaging in different activities. Yet as far as an Ireland moving towards independence was concerned, the Queen's tradition of patriotic melodrama clearly kept alight the torch of nationalism to a highly significant degree.

Shortly before his death in 1939, Yeats pondered the effect of his 1902 play *Cathleen ni Houlihan*, enquiring of himself '*Did that play of mine send out/Certain men the English shot?*' He was probably right to assume that it did; but his audience numbered only three hundred persons per night at the initial three-night run and sparse attendances thereafter. When one considers how many millions saw the patriotic melodramas in the commercial theatres over a quarter-century or more, one comes close to comprehending the true impact of the indigenous Irish drama on the national psyche. '*Did those plays by O'Grady, Whitbread, Fagan, Johnson, Mackey, etc., etc. send out/Certain men the English shot?*' The answer should be an uneqivocal '*Yes*'. What emerges here is the mutual non-comprehension of the two strands — the popular and the intellectual. The perpetrators of the popular had an excuse — their objective was to entertain a large public with whatever appealed, and what appealed was a theatre that looked forward to an independent Ireland, however much the concept was cloaked in bombast and blarney. There was less excuse for Yeats and his circle for misunderstanding — or really for ignoring — the strengths of the popular Irish theatre. Had they investigated companies like Kennedy Miller's or O'Grady's or Howard & Mackey's and solicited help with presentation, stage management, scenic construction (not to speak of diction, deportment and acting), all in the interests of building a theatre that was truly national — in other words if they had concentrated on the *writing* and left the technicalities to those who understood them — they would have achieved their aims with less discord and more dispatch.

PATRICK MALAHIDE AND DEARBHLA MOLLOY IN THE 2002
OUT OF JOINT-ABBEY THEATRE CO-PRODUCTION OF
SEBASTIAN BARRY'S *HINTERLAND*, DIRECTED BY MAX
STAFFORD-CLARK AND DESIGNED BY ES DEVLIN.

Photo: John Haynes.

NICHOLAS GRENE

PLAYS AND
CONTROVERSIES

'As an Irish Theatre, the Abbey's knell is rung,' wrote Joseph Holloway in his diary for 1 February 1907 in the wake of the riots over *The Playboy of the Western World*.[1] Holloway, architect of the Abbey and addicted play-goer, wrote with that gloomy satisfaction that has characterised many later prophecies of the Abbey's passing, all so far equally premature. It is hardly surprising that the Irish National Theatre should so often have been pronounced dead or dying. For, from very close to its beginnings, it has appeared bent on tearing itself apart.

The initial triumvirate of W.B. Yeats, Lady Gregory and Edward Martyn who thought up the Irish Literary Theatre in 1897 didn't stay together beyond their second season; Martyn was replaced by his outrageous cousin, the novelist

George Moore. Moore went almost as quickly when he and Yeats came to the verge of litigation over the property rights in a jointly conceived play. If Yeats, Gregory and John Synge, founding directors of the Abbey itself, remained in place, it may have been only because of Synge's early death in 1909, five years after the theatre opened. Synge had already been writing mutinous letters to his fiancée, Molly Algood, threatening to pull out, convinced that his fellow directors were hogging the show for themselves and their plays at his expense. When it came to the actors, there was a continuous round of secessions and walk-outs: some left early on political grounds, in protest at the theatre's lack of nationalist purpose; some, like the Fay brothers, the founders of the first acting company, because they would not accept the directors' dictatorial directorship.

Well, fights and factions, rows and resignations – that's theatre for you, in the boardroom and the greenroom as on stage. With the Abbey, however, it was and perhaps is still somewhat different. The Abbey's disputes have been aired as public controversies, whether as disagreements within the management, between the management and the company or, most dramatically, between the theatre and its audience. The conflicts have not just arisen due to the usual personal and professional rivalries or the vagaries of public taste, though these have no doubt played their part. The very conception of a national theatre in Ireland was a controversial one from the start.

The Irish Literary Theatre, as imagined by its creators, was in many ways an anti-commercial arthouse, like André Antoine's Théâtre Libre, set up in Paris in 1891, or the Moscow Art Theatre starting in 1898, just a year before the Irish Literary Theatre's first season. These were all small avant-garde ventures, intended to raise aesthetic standards in the theatre, aimed at minority audiences of like-minded souls. Yet the Irish Literary Theatre also claimed national status, rejecting colonial misrepresentation in its 1897 manifesto: 'we will show that Ireland is not the home of buffoonery and of easy sentiment, as it has been represented, but the home of an ancient idealism'. Its object, as the manifesto-writers stirringly put it, was 'to bring upon the stage the deeper thoughts and emotions of Ireland'.[2] To fulfil that ambition they needed to appeal to as wide and comprehensive an Irish audience as possible, not just an arthouse élite. And the audience was always liable to reject what was on offer, if it did not correspond to *their* idea of the 'deeper thoughts and emotions of Ireland'.

That was the case in the controversy over Yeats's *The Countess Cathleen*, performed in 1899, where the story of the self-sacrificing countess, who sells her soul to the devil to buy food for the starving peasants, was pronounced blasphemously un-Irish. This was the issue again with Synge's first produced play, *In the Shadow of the Glen* in 1903, which provoked protests by Maud Gonne and Arthur Griffith at the story of the young, unhappily married country woman leaving her husband for a tramp: a calumny on Irish womanhood, a foreign fabrication, foisting the spirit of the Latin Quarter on the people of Ireland. And these were only dress rehearsals for the *Playboy* riots.

The audience of the Abbey demanded that what was shown on the stage of their national theatre should be both representative and authentic. The controversy over *The Playboy* was a row over the real. Again and again the protesters complained that what was represented on stage as the behaviour of the people of Mayo was not true. And they frequently gave their credentials for these declarations of inauthenticity. So, for example, the person who wrote to *The Freeman's Journal* in shocked indignation at the use of the indelicate word 'shift' signed herself 'A Western Girl'.[3] This was a real-life Pegeen Mike who *knew* that no such person would ever utter such a word – 'even to herself'. In the theatre the shouts were often declarations of disbelief – 'That's not the West of Ireland.' It slightly backfired when Old Mahon's line about how Christy was 'a poor fellow would get drunk at the smell of a pint' produced the knee-jerk reaction, 'That's not Western life'[4] – laughter in court at this unintended defence of the western men's capacity to hold their drink. What was resented in Synge was the claim to authentic knowledge, the claim that he was able to represent the western country people truly and accurately. Lurking here, no doubt, was class and sectarian resentment that an Anglo-Irish Protestant, a mere tourist in the western counties, should imagine that he knew the people from the inside. That was why the reference to the chink in the floorboards in the Preface to *The Playboy* was so inflammatory: it only confirmed the nationalist conception of Synge as outsider, gentleman eavesdropper on the servant girls in the kitchen. Yeats might have advised Synge to go to the Aran Islands and 'live there as if you were one of the people themselves', but that was a long way from *being* one of the people themselves.

Allowing for this class animus and the political context, what was at stake for both sides was the authority of the real. Synge, on his side of the argument, claimed it just as stubbornly as his critics. Defending his earlier play *The Well of the Saints* against objections to some of its language from the Abbey actors, Synge asserted, 'What I write of Irish country life, I know to be true and I most emphatically will not change a syllable of it because A. B. or C. may think they know better than I do.'[5] What was at issue between Synge and the *Playboy* protesters was not the actual but the real, and reality is in the eye of the beholder. There is a telling passage from *The Aran Islands* that nicely illustrates the point. Synge is registering his sense of the mixed nature of his experience of island life, in spite of his enchantment with it:

> It is only in the intonation of a few sentences
> or some old fragments of melody that I catch
> the real spirit of the island, for in general the
> men sit together and talk with endless iteration
> of the tides and fish, and the price of kelp in
> Connemara.[6]

The tides and fish and the price of kelp in Connemara aren't *real?* Not to Synge they are not, even though they constitute the daily reality of these people who must live by the movement of the tides, live off the fish and selling kelp in the markets of Connemara.

These contested values of reality and authenticity in the early national theatre may reflect the need for cultural self-affirmation. A long-colonised people are forced to accept forms of identity from elsewhere: their culture, their behaviour, their very being is derived from the colonising centre. This is the perception of Stephen Dedalus when, in a famous passage of *A Portrait of the Artist as a Young Man*, he reflects on his knowledge of English as against that of the English-born Dean of Studies.

> The language in which we are speaking is his
> before it is mine. How different are the words
> *home, Christ, ale, master,* on his lips and on mine!
> I cannot speak or write those words without

unrest of spirit. His language, so familiar and
so foreign, will always be for me an acquired
speech.[7]

Given the insecurity of a colonised country, the lack of
self-belief that we are our own people, it may be
understandable that reality should be so important to us.
Somewhere, at some time in Ireland, there must be or
must have been a reality that is not merely an imported
culture shipped in off the mail-boat. Synge in writing his
plays believed he was in touch with such a reality; his
opponents vehemently insisted they knew better. But
both claimed privileged knowledge of the 'real spirit of
the island'. And this reality was something other than the
actuality of what went on day by day in the accidental life
of the here and now.

'You have disgraced yourselves *again*,' Yeats thundered
from the stage of the Abbey in 1926, when the audience
had rioted on the fourth night of O'Casey's *The Plough
and the Stars*; conscious that even his thundering might not
be heard over the din of the vociferous objectors, he
took care to have his speech written out in advance for
distribution to the newspapers. However, the row over
The Plough was not just a re-run of the *Playboy* riots, as
Yeats's 'again' implied. The circumstances were quite
different. In 1907 Synge's *Playboy* had been produced at
the national theatre of an emergent nation, provocatively
challenging its concept of nationhood. In 1926, ten
years after the Rising, O'Casey appeared to be calling in
question the ideals of the men who had given their lives
to achieve the independent Free State established in
1922. But of course that Free State itself was still a
contested manifestation of the nation. The row over *The
Plough* was a continuation of the civil war by other means,

with the battle-lines drawn between Free Staters and Republicans.

In the context of the time, it was significant that the year before, in 1925, the Abbey had been given its first subsidy by the Free State government, and Yeats – he of the thundering denunciation of the audience – was a Free State Senator who had supported the government in their draconian anti-Republican legislation. This gave the protesters a thick stick to beat the play and the theatre. 'The Free State government is subsidising the Abbey to malign Pearse and Connolly,' declared Hanna Sheehy-Skeffington, leading spokeswoman on the Republican side.[8]

Pearse and Connolly, the martyrs of 1916, were already by 1926 the universally acclaimed fathers of the nation. But for the Republicans the Free State as constituted in 1922 was not their legitimate child; it was a changeling substitute of a nation, not the true-born Republic that had been spirited away with the fairies. *The Plough*, that scurrilous misrepresentation of the Rising, was a typical product of a theatre sponsored by and in collusion with the ignoble imposter of an Irish Free State. As the living manifestation of this indignant charge, there in the audience at the Abbey on the explosive fourth night were the widowed mothers, wives, sisters of those martyred men of 1916: Mrs Pearse, mother of Patrick and Willie, Mrs Tom Clarke, Mrs Hanna Sheehy-Skeffington whose pacifist husband was shot by the British, though only trying to stop the looting. There can be little doubt that they were gathered there deliberately to provide a show of strength in the denunciation of the scandalous falsity of O'Casey's version of 1916. We were there; they were our husbands, sons, brothers who died for Ireland; what this Free State-subsidised theatre is showing is a grotesque travesty of the truth.

Once again the row produced ludicrous-seeming arguments over authenticity, turning particularly on the second act, with the notorious appearance of Rosie Redmond the prostitute. Prostitutes: there were no such people in the holy city of Dublin. Come again? It is also in this act that Lieutenant Langon carries the Tricolour into the pub and drinks a sacred toast to the revolution. The Tricolour, claimed the protesters, was never seen inside a licensed premises. It is easy to laugh now at the hysterics and histrionics of the controversy. What was felt at the time was a need for a complete identity between the sacred and the real. Easter 1916, the foundational act in the creation of a new Ireland, was a sacred drama, played out as such by the leaders with a full sense of the symbolic and the theatrical: in the choice of Easter as a date, in the occupation of the GPO right across from Nelson's Pillar, centre of Ireland's capital city, in the reading out of the proclamation before those imposing neoclassical pillars. But it was a sacred drama acted out by real men in a real theatre of war, bringing with it a transformation of ordinary, everyday reality that no one ever expressed better than Yeats in his poem 'Easter 1916'. The men he encountered coming from counter or desk amid grey eighteenth century houses, the men of the casual comedy, were changed, changed utterly. In that moment of transubstantiation, it was essential for true believers to believe both in the reality of the bread and wine and of the Real Presence of God-ordained revolution. And here was O'Casey, Protestant that he was – though to be fair to his antagonists that was *never* used against him – denying the Real Presence, dramatising instead an inchoate human reality untouched by the sacred, unredeemed by the Rising.

There continued to be controversies over the suitability of the plays staged by the National Theatre in later years. In 1933 the Abbey's tour of North America was put in danger when Irish American organisations objected to its repertory; its plays, the directors were told, were 'open to serious objections on various grounds', 'filthy language, drunkenness, murder and prostitution, and holding up the Irish character generally to be scoffed at'.[9] Ironically, within Ireland, *The Playboy* and *The Plough* had become accepted as popular classics, as indeed they were for most American audiences; only some greener than green Irish Americans were still fighting the good fight against them. The incident could have had serious consequences for the theatre – a reduction of the government subsidy, much greater state control. But some resolute defending on the part of Yeats and some skilful diplomatic footwork on the part of de Valera, head of the Fianna Fáil government elected for the first time the previous year, brought a negotiated compromise.

Yeats's own playwriting career in Ireland ended, as it had begun, in controversy. His strange late play *The Herne's Egg* was thought too obscene to be staged at the Abbey; and with a central incident in which seven wandering knights rape the priestess Attracta, one can see that it might have raised some eyebrows. *Purgatory*, produced in 1938 in the last summer of Yeats's life in a special festival of Abbey drama, provoked immediate criticism for its heterodox theology. Yeats remained defiant to the last: 'I wish to say', he declared from the stage after the opening performance, 'that I have put into this play not many thoughts that are picturesque but my own beliefs about this world and the next.'[10] Thirty-nine years after

The Countess Cathleen the poet was still unrepentant in the face of charges of blasphemy or heresy, still unwilling to adjust his own vision to that of his audience.

There has been no shortage of objections to the staging of this or that play at the Abbey, right down to 2002 with the strong press reactions against Sebastian Barry's *Hinterland* for its use of an obviously identifiable living individual as model for its central character. But from the 1920s on, many of the arguments have been about what the Abbey has *not* put on. Two of the most publicised instances came in the same year, 1928, with the rejection of Denis Johnston's *The Old Lady Says No!* and O'Casey's *The Silver Tassie*.

This is often taken to be the moment at which the shutters came down at the Abbey; a movement that had originally claimed for itself that 'freedom to experiment which is not found in the theatres of England' now turned its back on that ideal and fossilised into a narrowly conservative national institution. It is certainly true that Yeats and Gregory had little time for the expressionist style of Johnston's play, though in the event Irish theatre was well served by their turning it down. The 1920s Abbey would not have had the skills and resources to give *The Old Lady Says No!* the production it needed, whereas for the newly founded Gate Theatre of Hilton Edwards and Micheál MacLíammóir it provided a brilliant inaugural showcase of their talents. For the rejection of *The Silver Tassie* there is much less to be said. Whatever the problems of the play, the Abbey owed O'Casey a staging of it, and so apparently both Lady Gregory and Lennox Robinson felt. It was Yeats who was responsible for turning it down, in a letter that combined wrong-headedness and high-handedness in almost equal measure: 'You are not interested in the Great War,' Yeats told O'Casey, 'you have never stood on its battlefields, never walked its hospitals, and so write out of your opinions.'[11] It was Yeats who had no interest in the Great War, and was notoriously to exclude the war poets from his *Oxford Book of Modern Verse*. O'Casey, never a man to resist a quarrel, had the whole correspondence between himself and the directors published in the press. The Abbey appeared to have deliberately, obtusely cast off their most famous and most popular playwright.

The name of Ernest Blythe, managing director of the Abbey from 1941 to 1967, is often associated with the most nay-saying phase of the theatre's history, the period at which it was claimed no play could be accepted without its quotient of p. q. – 'peasant quality'. Blythe's attempt to make of the Abbey an Irish-language theatre was doomed to failure, though it did result in the recruitment of two of the Abbey's best directors, Frank Dermody and Tomás Mac Anna. The programming from this period was for the most part unadventurous and there were some notable rejections by Blythe himself. According to one version of the story he not only turned down but also physically threw the script of *The Quare Fellow* back at Brendan Behan.[12] When Tom Murphy submitted his first full-length play, *A Whistle in the Dark*, to the Abbey, he received not just a rejection from Blythe but also 'an abusive denunciation. The characters of the play, he said, were unreal, and its atmosphere was incredible. He did not believe that such people as were to appear in *A Whistle* existed in Ireland.'[13] Back to authenticity: the national theatre should not stage any but nationally representative figures.

Behan and Murphy both went on to major success in London with the plays contemptuously rejected by the Abbey. Yet both playwrights were to be staged at the Irish

National Theatre eventually. This has been the pattern with many of the theatre's most celebrated rejects. Shaw's *John Bull's Other Island* might have been the Abbey's opening production in 1904, but it was not thought suitable or indeed feasible with the resources available to the infant company. It was produced by the Abbey eventually in 1916 and thereafter became one of the most frequently revived plays in their repertoire for many years to come. In spite of all the publicity over the rejection of *The Silver Tassie*, it did receive an Abbey staging in 1935. So it was with Behan and Murphy. *The Quare Fellow*, so violently flung back at Behan originally, with the following wind of its popular London production, was successfully put on in the Abbey in 1956. The theatre, if only belatedly, has shown itself capable of learning by its mistakes.

The case of Murphy is an even more striking one. After the major 1961 success of *A Whistle in the Dark* in London, which encouraged him to move there and become a full-time writer, Murphy's career did not altogether take off. It was not until the end of the decade, with landmark productions at the Abbey of his plays *Famine* and *A Crucial Week in the Life of a Grocer's Assistant*, that Murphy's reputation became fully established. It was the Abbey that staged his most radically experimental plays of the 1970s, *The Morning after Optimism* and *The Sanctuary Lamp*, *The Sanctuary Lamp* one of the last plays in the Abbey to raise objections at its anti-clericalism. *The Gigli Concert* is now accepted as one of the theatre's classic plays, to be revived and toured in the Abbey's centenary season. But when it was first staged in 1983 it was regarded as a high-risk piece, which Joe Dowling, the then artistic director, insisted on having produced in the face of strong opposition from his own board, and which was initially received with a high degree of critical incomprehension.

The history of the plays the Abbey has turned down and its institutional position as national theatre have resulted in a lingering public perception of it as a stultified monument to its own past greatness, unreceptive to new playwrights, impenetrable by new ideas. A look back over the last thirty years of the company's work should correct that impression. Thomas Kilroy's *Talbot's Box*, at the Peacock in 1977, gave to a strikingly original play the strikingly original staging it needed. Brian Friel's *Faith Healer*, a calamitous failure when it opened in New York in 1979, was triumphantly successful at the Abbey the following year with Donal McCann in the lead. It was apparently *Faith Healer* that inspired Frank McGuinness to become a playwright; and it was the Abbey that staged his first play *The Factory Girls* in 1982 and then the landmark *Observe the Sons of Ulster Marching towards the Somme* in 1985. The 1980s also saw *The Great Hunger*, the movement-based adaptation of Kavanagh's poem by Tom McIntyre. With the proliferation of theatre companies in Ireland, and lucrative opportunities for Irish playwrights in London, there have been some striking cases of ones that got away, like the spectacularly successful Conor McPherson and Martin McDonagh, whose work was not premièred by the Abbey. Against that has to be set the list of those whose plays have been nurtured by the National Theatre: Frank McGuinness, Sebastian Barry, Marina Carr, Eugene O'Brien.

To claim the status of a national theatre is to set yourself up for criticism by the nation you claim to represent. And the artistic director has come to be the first in the firing-line. While Yeats remained a director from the theatre's foundation to his death in 1939, and Blythe for over twenty-five years, there have been times since when tenure of the artistic directorship of the

Abbey has been about as secure as life-expectancy on the western front in World War I. The artistic director is berated when there are not enough new plays; he or she is lambasted when the new plays put on do not succeed. It is not much easier when it comes to revivals either. Two instances from the 1990s can be used to illustrate the point.

Garry Hynes was appointed artistic director in 1991, having made her reputation with the Druid Theatre company she had helped to found in Galway. Her inaugural production as director was a radically re-conceived *Plough and the Stars* in an expressionist style: a non-representational setting, actors with shaven heads and stylised make-up, the lines of Patrick Pearse, normally spoken by a silhouette in the window of act two, delivered by an actor planted in the audience. Many of the reviews were admiring, with headlines like 'A mould breaking debut of courage' and 'Hynes' *Plough* makes fresh statements'.[14] But there was also an outraged reaction from others: 'What we're being offered is ... yesterday's avant-garde';[15] 'O'Casey's greatest play has been squeezed dry of all its life and fun and passion'.[16] A lively correspondence followed in *The Irish Times*, not all of it negative by any means, but the negative parts of it damaged the play at the box-office. Audiences were not willing to forego their familiar O'Casey, the droll Dublin accents, the dear, dirty tenement scenes.

When Patrick Mason took over the artistic directorship in 1994, his first show was a strikingly innovative production of Synge's *The Well of the Saints*. In this case, his direction was generally admired, but his judgement in choosing to stage the play was called into question. At best there was the damning sound of faint praise: 'This may not prove everyone's cup of theatrical tea, but it is a significant reworking of a minor Abbey Theatre classic for our times.'[17] More often there was simple dismissal: 'here is a play that should simply not have been put on at all'.[18] When the production was taken to the Edinburgh Festival the reaction was very different. It was greeted with a chorus of praise and given the critics' award for best dramatic production, before going on to an equally successful reception in Australia.

A national theatre is a national Aunt Sally: it's our taxpayers' money that goes to support it, so we are all entitled to have a go at it. Fair enough. The history of the Abbey is a history of plays and controversies, of a continuing capacity for self-laceration and an equally continuing capacity for self-renewal. In celebrating its centenary, we celebrate the spirit of contentiousness that has driven people to argue about what we are as a nation and what should constitute our national theatre. The one danger is mere indifference: it's not worth bothering about, leave it be as a cultural heritage centre for bussed-in tourists, a museum monument to its founders. It's not a very great danger, though. With ambitious playwrights, actors, directors and designers still aspiring to work in what remains Ireland's prestige theatre, with captious critics there to criticise and pundits to pontificate, it will, with a bit of luck, be a few years yet before the knell of the Abbey is rung.

Notes

[1] Robert Hogan and Michael J. O'Neill (eds), *Joseph Holloway's Abbey Theatre* (Carbondale and Edwardsville: Southern Illinois University Press; London and Amsterdam: Feffer & Simons, 1967), p. 86.

[2] Quoted in Lady Gregory, *Our Irish Theatre* (Gerrards Cross: Colin Smythe, 3rd ed., 1972), p. 20.

[3] James Kilroy, *The 'Playboy' Riots* (Dublin: Dolmen Press, 1971), p. 10.

[4] Christopher Morash, 'All Playboys Now: the Audience and the Riot', in Nicholas Grene (ed.), *Interpreting Synge: Essays from the Synge Summer School 1991–2000* (Dublin: Lilliput Press, 2000), p. 143.

[5] Ann Saddlemyer, Introduction, J.M. Synge, *Collected Works, III: Plays*, Book I (London: Oxford University Press, 1968), p. xxiv.

[6] J.M. Synge, *Collected Works, II: Prose*, ed. Alan Price (London: Oxford University Press, 1966), p. 74.

[7] James Joyce, *A Portrait of the Artist as a Young Man* (London: Secker & Warburg, 1994), pp. 198–9.

[8] Quoted in Nicholas Grene, *The Politics of Irish Drama* (Cambridge: Cambridge University Press, 1999), p. 140.

[9] Cited by R.F. Foster, *W.B. Yeats: a Life* vol. II *The Arch-Poet* (Oxford: Oxford University Press, 2003), p. 464

[10] Ibid., p. 628.

[11] Quoted in Robert Welch, *The Abbey Theatre 1899–1999: Form and Pressure* (Oxford: Oxford University Press, 1999), p. 107.

[12] See Michael O'Sullivan, *Brendan Behan: a Life* (Dublin: Blackwater Press, 1997), p. 178.

[13] Fintan O'Toole, *The Politics of Magic: the Work and Times of Tom Murphy* (Dublin: Raven Arts Press, 1987), p. 42.

[14] *Irish Independent*, 8 May 1991; *Evening Press*, 8 May 1991.

[15] Fergus Linehan, 'Second Opinion', *The Irish Times*, 11 May 1991.

[16] Hugh Leonard, 'The Plough and the Starved', *Sunday Independent*, 19 May 1991.

[17] David Nowlan, *The Irish Times*, 9 June 1994.

[18] Lorcan Roche, *Irish Independent*, 9 June 1994.

JONATHAN ARUN AND DARRAGH KELLY IN THE 1995
ABBEY THEATRE PRODUCTION OF TONY KUSHNER'S
ANGELS IN AMERICA, DIRECTED BY PATRICK MASON
AND DESIGNED BY JOE VANEK.

Abbey National Theatre Archives. Photo: Amelia Stein.

EMER O'KELLY

THE MIRROR CRACK'D:
REFRACTIONS FROM
CRITICISM

In this year when we celebrate the
centenary of the Abbey, our National
Theatre, the time has come for those of
us involved in criticism to hold up our
hands and admit that for much of the
past hundred years what has passed for
criticism has had little to do with
detached observance putting the theatre's
work into a framework of international
theatrical development. Review was, and
indeed to this day sometimes is, the best
that could be hoped for. Analysis of a
particular theatrical form, its genesis and
its quality in terms of a world theatre
movement, was ignored as irrelevant, even
at times as antagonistic to something that
was more 'part of what we are' than an
element of an art form that has been with
humanity for thousands of years. Over
the century of the Abbey's existence,

criticism was debased to the personal and the parochial, even among those who might have been expected to be detached observers.

T.S. Eliot believed in the critical principle that the past should be altered by the present, as much as the present is directed by the past. He believed that literature, including drama, was subject to a kind of existing order in the framework of European art. In parallel terms, he believed that the artist should have a sense of tradition to make it possible to come to terms with the totality of written art: it was, he posited, an organic whole, rather than a collection of individual works, or even the composite of different streams of national cultures. In other words, the artist owes allegiance to something beyond individual vision. Eliot, of course, was writing of the artist as professional critic, but his argument holds equally for the critic *per se*, who is there to elucidate and analyse the artist's work.

But Eliot also believed that there is no such thing as original art, because no single work of art exists in isolation. The great artists are all consumed with an awareness of what has brought them to the making of their own art, and therefore all art is in part a configuration of what has gone before, and a stage on the road towards what will come in the future. In other words, criticism in its truest form and at the highest level finds its fulfilment outside itself, actually in a union with the creativity of the artist. This comes about when the critic stands aside from the personal and engages objectively with the piece of art as a prism of reflection as well as an intrinsically glinting object. This in itself explains and indeed justifies the frequency with which artists, be they novelists, poets or playwrights, engage in the commercial form of criticism of each other's work, as opposed to an enclosed critical debate within their own ranks (as was the case with Eliot and the rest of the Bloomsbury set). Nowadays, artists who cross the line into criticism are likely to find themselves accused of being members of an incestuous old boys' or girls' club, and when the commercial criticism is less than rigorous the accusation is justified. But at the higher, and paradoxically more visceral, levels they are engaged in reflecting their own practice in the prism of fellow artists' work. Yet when it comes from one who is primarily an artist, criticism loses its analytical purity to the necessary process of the artist's personal vision.

Criticism must be concerned with fact above all; and fact can become blurred when one is inside the prism that is art. The critic's first function is to analyse the work in objective terms; in other words, to pick its bones to assess its quality within its own firmament. That done, the critic's job is to return the layers of qualitative flesh by means of comparison with like and previous work. This is frequently the more dangerous of the two functions, because comparative judgements are often influenced by personal taste and preferences, both areas with which the critic should strive not to be concerned. If they are not avoided, criticism can come down to a basic level of exclusion: the critic can find him or herself making judgements on the grounds of personal enjoyment. 'I liked this; therefore it is good.' 'I do not like that particular genre, or I despise that particular genre; therefore this production is bad because it is in that genre.' Thus in terms of objective criticism, the fellow artist, or indeed the aspiring artist within a particular form, is not the best and most detached critic, and better serves the art form in which he or she is involved with, or aspires to be involved with, by avoiding the critic's role.

An aspiring playwright or a fellow novelist is not best qualified to judge a play or a novel.

Equally, the professional critic can be less than pure in approach. Indeed, until comparatively recently (as I said initially) critics working in Ireland were expected to share the principles and views of the sector of society which read the publication in which their work appeared. It was seen as their employed duty to reflect the views of their readers and listeners, rather than leading or forming them. And by and large, they did. Newspaper publishing was less open than it is now to a broad spectrum of opinion and influences, and critics were expected to bow to the overall socio-economic/cultural policy of their employment house, although this was not perhaps as entirely objectionable as it might seem at first glance. We live in a small society in Ireland, and readers of newspapers and magazines have always felt a kind of attachment to the writers whose work they read. It is easy for anyone to walk down Abbey Street or D'Olier Street in Dublin and see the luminaries of *The Irish Times* or the various Independent newspapers going in and out of their buildings. But just as until comparatively recently the *Irish Independent* was seen as a bastion of Roman Catholic orthodoxy and *The Irish Times* a bastion of Protestant (and therefore, it was assumed, liberal) philosophy, it was expected that their critics would write from those perspectives. A critic working from Independent House would never fully outrage Catholic opinion and sensibilities; the farthest he might go would be to express an opinion that might be seen as vaguely anti-clerical, but it would be from within the safety net of broad Catholic orthodoxy. In those days, when *The Irish Times* was a bastion of empire loyalism and embattled Protestantism, *those* orthodoxies would not be undermined in the paper's columns: mild guying of the more extreme forms would be the closest a critic would come to subversive independence. Objectivity was not required, reinforcement was the code of practice and the critics were unfortunately quite happy to go along with this. And in many cases they went along not because it was overtly required of them, but because such views were their own in the first place. Objectivity, that first marker for the critic, was not a consideration. The overall policy in these two cases was not changed until the Independent group went out of the hands of the Catholic conservative family, the Murphys, and Douglas Gageby as editor of *The Irish Times* took an editorial decision to support the Fianna Fáil party in a general election and urge the paper's readers to vote for that party's policies.

In some cases the stranglehold of critical orthodoxy (which is actually a reduction to personally prejudiced reviews) has still not changed, although in most cases it has. It is only a few years since someone calling himself a critic (although not now working in that field) said to me that, as far as he was concerned, a certain play should not have been staged in Dublin because its theme was blasphemous and therefore innately immoral. The man was in his twenties and saw himself as a liberal. He saw no reason to explain the limits to his liberalism (although it clashed with his core prejudices) and went on to give the play a very poor review. It deserved it; it was a very bad play – but that was not the trigger for the judgement being made. Two of the major laws of criticism had been broken: one, the striving for objectivity; two, the non-statement of the critic's rules of engagement. The critic is not a moral arbiter: one can state that a play's theme strikes one as immoral, but one must put the statement in the context of explaining one's own moral code. Morality is not a fixed point. Above all, it is against all the laws of criticism for the critic to assume that the personal view is the objective truth: when he or she does, it becomes an exercise in narcissism, and a bigoted one at that.

But such attitudes were almost universal in Irish criticism for most of the twentieth century. They were not challenged, because the critic was a member of the same club as his or her audience. Theatre-goers were divided into those who wanted a good evening out, without being asked to think too much about what they saw, and those who were prepared to have their minds stimulated. But even the stimulation ran along pre-disposed lines. When 'the Abbey Theatre opened its doors in 1904, people knew what to expect, or they should have. The theatre's founders were already engaged in idealising Ireland, her culture and her people. Above all, they had a specific political purpose in representing Ireland to its people as a victimised society. Yeats and Lady Gregory may not have shared the simplistic nationalist code that was to become the orthodoxy in the 1920s and later, but they did see Irish culture as a victim of colonialism. And they were nationalistic enough, or at least Yeats was, to believe that Irish culture and its folk tradition were vastly superior to much of the great body of world art throughout history, remaining unacknowledged as such only because of repression. Yeats was, in fact, an identifiable precursor of Brian Friel's contemptuous hedge schoolmaster in *Translations*. It was only from within the broad family of contemptuous nationalist superiority that they were prepared to outrage popular opinion. Fundamentally, they were at one with even the most severe of their critics.

The Abbey founders fed in to a national con-sciousness ill-equipped and unwilling to engage in rigorous cultural debate. Irish superiority was a given; that this was not recognised universally was the fault of the conqueror. It was a classic state of victimhood, and one the then critics were happy to endorse. The early plays were not seen as pieces of art, but rather as personifications of what the country wanted to see as its identity. That, in part, explains the sense of outrage that led to the *Plough and the Stars* riots. The people had indeed disgraced themselves again, as Yeats told them. But he was the only one who said it; critical opinion in the capital city was on the side of the rioters. There was a national unwillingness among the people who should have been leading critical thought to engage in anything fundamentally challenging to the received political and religious wisdom of the day.

In fact, far from being a national theatre, the early Abbey was not only not national, it was not even a theatre, as George Bernard Shaw noted from many perspectives. Writing as late as the 1930s, he said that the Abbey Theatre was a 'noble endeavour' but had never been and never would be a theatre. And at the time he was right, because the Abbey's major purpose was to be a leader of 'the national movement', a sacred endeavour somewhat detached from the basic task of making art. That it would better serve that declared purpose, as well as what should be the purpose of a theatre, by dedicating itself to real independence of spirit and opening its doors to international influences and thought did not occur to its founders. In that, they were very much a part of the Irish national consciousness, despite their arrogant assumptions of being above it. To be Irish at the time meant to refuse to criticise; it was to turn a blind eye to any faults in the national psyche. Criticism was considered base, negative and unpatriotic. In addition, anything that was part of the narrow definition of what was truly 'Irish' had to be gilded to give it an idealised aura.

That was true even when O'Casey's three great tenement plays were being heralded for the revolutionary quality of their gritty realism. His socialist passion was quickly eroded by the *manner* in which his plays were produced. They became hymns to the very thing that he was railing against – narrow Irish nationalism and the glorification of armed struggle – when their author meant them as passionate protests against the futility of war and the repression exerted by religious authority. It was an early form of the dumbing-down that is now so objected to in television programming. It was understandable that general public opinion should accept this new 'official' version of O'Casey's work as he turned his back in disgust on Ireland's narrowing horizons; it was under the sway of a whole new movement spearheaded by a government which was rewriting the recent history of the country and painting the 1916 Rising as springing from a great popular movement, meanwhile whitewashing *out* of history the thousands of young men who had gone to the Great War. They had come back to be told that they were not 'real' Irishmen, and lived on, damaged in mind and body, in a society which had redefined patriotism, culture and Irishness. Their officer class, the educated middle-class young men, found themselves even more isolated. A new war had been declared, and it was against them, as their families' houses were burned down, and they found themselves classified as oppressors of the communities in which they had spent their lives. Not surprisingly, many of them turned their backs on the Ireland they had always loved: they no longer saw themselves as having any place here, as literature, theatre and the professions became subsumed into a nationalist élite from which there could be no dissent.

Ireland was now being run by what Tod Andrews in his memoir in old age was to call 'the men of no property'. So property and its appurtenances, the old civilisations of broad education and the fine arts, became, almost by definition, something risible in the new Ireland. In parallel with this unhealthy nationalist élitism in theatre and other arts there was a closing down of our cultural borders through the mechanisms of censorship, so that very little of what was happening on the cultural scene in Britain and the rest of Europe, much less in the United States, was permitted to break through. And given the rarity of foreign travel in those poverty-stricken times before the advent of cheap and easy transport, very few Irish citizens travelled. There was nobody to bring back the exciting news of world theatre and the world of international books and the visual arts. Ireland was existing in a suffocating critical bubble, with those who should have been the leaders of debate acquiescing in the new determinism that defined Ireland in terms of not being English. And, of course, there were no comparative standards, the easy epithet of 'common knowledge', that is, the uninformed prejudice of the majority, being infinitely preferable to any kind of genuine critical analysis based on fact.

We still suffer from that hangover: critical analysis in certain areas of the arts is seen as post-colonial inferiority complex, while there is also a school of opinion which defines folk art forms as intrinsically superior to the fine arts because they are indigenous. And while folk art is undoubtedly part of what we are, it is *only* part, and our critical abilities as a nation, as well the whole school of professional critical analysis, can only be damaged by such a reactionary and defensive view of the arts. The real post-colonial inferiority complex lies in an attitude that sees the art of Ireland in isolation, as a stand-alone entity that neither has been nor needs to be influenced from outside our shores. This is defined by refusing to see the limitations of certain kinds of artistry produced in this country, as, for instance, in the early days of the Abbey, when the highly naturalistic 'peasant' style of acting was seen as a matter of deliberate choice rather than as an inevitable product of a complete lack of professional training. That it was hugely limiting in terms of the artistic choices the company could make was ignored by those who concentrated on its uniqueness, which was indeed refreshingly different from the mannered style of 'high art' acting then in vogue. But from that acceptance it was an easy critical step to considering it superior simply because it was Irish.

Only, however, if it was a form of idealised stage-Irishry. When the Abbey toured Synge's *Playboy* to the United States for the first time it provoked much the same reaction as it had at home, being reviewed by the Irish American press in the highly defensive terms of nationalistic sentiment: it was obvious, one reviewer suggested, that this slur on Irish nobility of character was in fact a demonic English plot. This could be proven, the reviewer said, because no Irish woman would have demeaned herself by traducing her country so, and could also be proven by the actresses' large feet. Everyone knew, he wrote, that all Irish women have particularly dainty feet. Misty-eyed emigrant memory is notoriously unreliable, but critical writing at home was equally defensive and continued to be. Most critics were in fact merely reviewers — something that remains the case in many areas. The early theatre reviewers of the twentieth century may not necessarily have been given to over-indulgence in alcohol, but they might as well have stayed in the bar and written their reviews from there for all the context and analysis used in their thought processes. It was the received wisdom that F.J. McCormick never gave less than a world-class performance, and he was so credited in the public mind each time he appeared on stage. It may well have been true, but the qualitative decision usually gave all the appearances of having been made before the loosely styled critic even left his office. And while Barry FitzGerald may have been much-loved playing Irish leprechaun priests in his later years in Hollywood, those performances do not lead one to believe in his classical versatility during his Abbey career, any more than Sarah Allgood deserved the misty recollections of having been a true *grande dame* of the Irish theatre. Her Hollywood career was limited to playing cooks and Irish immigrant mothers in the slums – all monotonous, and in an accent of strangulated refinement.

In the much more recent past, some of the actors of my teenage theatre-going days are spoken of with awe nowadays as having been part of a kind of theatrical dream machine. But I can remember a number of them frequently being visibly drunk on stage, and at least two of them, even to my then untutored eye, regularly gave performances coated in matchless layers of ham, and were incapable of remembering lines of parts which they had played in excess of a dozen times.

This talk is concerned mainly with criticism as it affected or did not affect the Abbey Theatre through its hundred-year history, but the Gate Theatre frequently got away with critical murder aswell. Its choice of plays may have been more challenging than the Abbey's during the early years, but it too had its share of potboilers, badly produced, badly directed and tattily costumed. But acceptance was formulaic. Those who favoured the Abbey claimed the Gate was moribund in its middle-class smugness; the Gate's champions condemned the Old Lady of Marlborough Street as existing in a twilight of the Celtic gods reduced to a farm-kitchen set. And both, indeed, had a point, although there was no critical voice to rise above the parochial and provide an international context and an intellectually focused debate on the purpose and quality of theatre.

In living memory, the critic of one major newspaper frequently stayed in the bar after the first interval on the basis that he knew the play and indeed the performances so well that he could write his review blind drunk, whatever theatre he was in. And he frequently did. That he was doing a grave disservice to the actors in whose inept work he was colluding never seems to have occurred to him or to anyone else. There was a *status quo* of opinion, none of it rigorous, its political awareness limited to the party politics of the day, if it existed at all. The theatre was seen as existing in a detached bubble, something separate from national life as it was developing. When the Northern Ireland troubles began, there was an attempt on the Peacock stage to produce a polemical revue encompassing recent as well as more ancient Irish history. The reaction to that was a microcosm of the way the Irish public viewed its theatre and expected its professional critics to reflect those views. The journalist Eamonn McCann, then a nationalist student activist at Queen's, rallied his Northern Ireland troops, and the stage was rushed in an attempt to stop the performance. There was a further narrow cosiness in that local Northern Ireland television had been alerted and was there to record the 'audience outrage'.

It was the 1970s, with barriers coming down

everywhere internationally; but closed nationalist bigotry was still demanded of theatre in Ireland — that, or soothing and glossy comedies of manners. That had changed radically within twenty years. In the 1990s, Patrick Mason as artistic director of the Abbey was able to stage Tony Kushner's *Angels in America*. Not only was it a breakthrough for a major international success to receive an Abbey production, but the play's content was serious and controversial, dealing as it did with the then Aids crisis and the unpleasant career of Hoover, the homosexual, right-wing head of America's FBI. The play also featured a scene of graphic and brutal homosexual sex. Only one person left on the opening night, and no critic found it necessary to dwell on the brief scene or on the walk-out. Criticism, it seemed, had finally come of age, along with the sensibilities of Irish theatre audiences.

It remains to be argued whether the more adult sensibilities of the Irish theatre-going public have demanded more mature and wide-ranging critical understanding of theatre, or whether criticism has itself contributed to the more stimulating diet of theatre available in the country. But Irish criticism and the theatre itself are now part of the world in which we operate, not just as a nation, but also as part of a fast-changing international spectrum. And as long as we increase our critical awareness over our tendency to self-congratulation, the future looks hopeful.

DUBLIN GATE THEATRE

PRODUCTIONS

WHERE STARS WALK

A Play in Three Acts by

MICHEÁL MAC LIAMMÓIR

PRESENTED BY

**HILTON EDWARDS AND
MICHEÁL MacLIAMMÓIR**

May. 1945

PROGRAMME COVER FOR A REVIVAL OF *WHERE
STARS WALK* BY MICHEÁL MACLÍAMMÓIR AT
THE DUBLIN GATE THEATRE IN 1945,
DIRECTED BY HILTON EDWARDS.

CHRISTOPHER MURRAY

'WHERE ARE THEY
NOW?': PLAYS OF
SIGNIFICANCE IN THE
1940S AND 1950S

It is common enough to hear the
argument that once Yeats died in January
1939 the Abbey died with him.[1] Like
most generalisations this one is
unreliable. For the theatre did not die, not
then nor even in 1951 when it was
attacked by fire in the small hours of a
July morning. It soldiered on until a new
building was built and opened in 1966
and it is soldiering on today, even while
another new building is under con-
templation. Yet those who advance the
charge that the Abbey died with Yeats
don't actually mean that the building
itself collapsed around him to form some
kind of mausoleum; they really refer to
artistic standards and to the production
of new plays capable of standing
comparison with those of the early and
great days.[2] In that regard the question is

debatable. Because the glory days were certainly over. O'Casey was gone into exile; his most promising successor, Paul Vincent Carroll, had been shabbily treated over his new play (*The White Steed*) in 1938 and took himself off also to Britain and pastures new; Denis Johnston left the theatre for the BBC once World War II broke out and for many years was lost to the Irish theatre. So who was left or who emerged to fill the ranks? It is my contention here that there were lots of writers who emerged or who blossomed at this time, though very few who have stood the awful test of time in the same way as Synge, O'Casey and the others from an earlier generation. But it is equally my contention that in the theatre nothing is really ever lost but while it gathers to itself the energies and themes from what went before it also generates new energies and new themes, even of lesser intensity, which in turn activate and in various ways reappear like ghosts in the perhaps greater plays which follow on in the next generation. That is to say, more briefly, that the history of theatre in a compact nation like Ireland is genetic. To change the metaphor, theatre history is a kind of endless unfolding of a huge roll of multi-coloured cloth, the pattern reappearing and reconnecting. So, in this talk, while I shall be asking 'where are they now?' and referring to the plays our fathers and mothers and possibly our grandfathers and grandmothers left the fireside and the kids to take the bus or tram to see and thought themselves well served, I hope to be able to show that these plays are in a rather uncanny way still with us.

As a way in to this subject I want first to mention a play staged not at the Abbey at all but at the Gaiety in 1940, *Where Stars Walk* by Micheál MacLíammóir. Two things about this piece are worth noting here. In the first place it is a sophisticated recycling of a Celtic myth, the love story of Etáin and Midhir, in the context of fashionable Dublin society at the time of performance. Cleverly, MacLíammóir sets the story, whereby a simple servant girl and determined manservant discover as if in a dream that they are in actuality the mythic lovers, against a background of a play being put on with this very theme. Illusion and reality are thus held up to scrutiny in ways which reinforce the very nature of theatre itself. Very well, Pirandello had done this sort of thing in more complex ways already on the international stage but this doing it Irish-style made a bridge between the mythic and the actual in ways that keep faith with ordinary life. The idea of the return of mythic folk is whimsical, no doubt, but it serves to represent also the very way plays work, recycling other writers as MacLíammóir recycled Yeats, and showing how a play is no more than an echo from the past which alerts and estranges the present. The other thing about *Where Stars Walk* is really a variation on this point. It is something MacLíammóir himself said in his preface to the printed text:

> [A]s the Nazi war on Europe became a more and more ominous reality [I realised] that the day of speculative romanticism was at its lowest ebb in the theatre. Not that it was dead, I said to myself, for I believed then, and perhaps I still believe, that *fashions in the arts do not pass forever out of existence*; they recede and advance like the tides; they vanish and reappear a little differently in shape, it may be, as Etáin herself had vanished and reappeared in that old story of her many deaths and births.[3]

Here, then, is my theme in relation to mid-century Irish drama, that such as it was it was rooted in tradition

and served in time to revisit or even to haunt another age,
no doubt for better or worse. It is at least worth
considering how MacLíammóir, that great illusionist,
that confidence man capable of passing himself off as
more Celtic than the Celts themselves, by his very
considerable presence in mid-century Ireland carried
through his own project to perfection and showed us all
how the question of identity is at bottom a theatrical one.

Over at the Abbey itself in the early 1940s all was in
process of change. The heyday of Lennox Robinson and
his sprightly comedies, such as *Drama at Inish* (1932), was
gone; likewise T.C. Murray's depiction of life as at best an
autumn fire had dwindled well before his death in 1959.
Yeats's successor as managing director, the poet F.R.
Higgins, while calling for new work, warned against the
danger of writers' looking at life 'through the eyes of the
Abbey stage',[4] an interesting admonition which gives us
one good reason why many of the plays of that time are
forgotten: they confused art, or convention, with life and
ended up being only artificial. When Higgins died
suddenly in January 1941 his place was taken by Ernest
Blythe, who proved much more durable: until 1967 in fact.
Blythe too wanted new plays but he also wanted full
houses, after which he could inflict plays in Irish on
captive audiences. The combination says a lot about the
public patience of the day. In effect Blythe allowed and
indeed fostered the long run at the Abbey, and to that end
he encouraged populism. He had a peculiar notion of
dramatic art, that it should have 'a constructive influence
on public affairs', implying propaganda of some kind,
though Blythe never engaged openly in same. Part of what
he was after is contained in his stated preference for a
theatre where issues which might otherwise be 'sources of
misunderstanding and division' could be 'combed out on

the stage and rendered innocuous by thorough ventilation there'.[5] The phrase 'rendered innocuous' is a telling one: Blythe was a long way from conceiving a *Late Late Show* style of debating forum, much less a theatre which allowed riots as in Yeats's day. Hence the prevalence of the happy ending in Abbey plays all through the 1940s and '50s. However serious the issues explored might be, the form must somehow contrive in the end to render them innocuous. Theatre was thus a social safety valve and, rivalling the film industry of that era, the provider of escapism.

For all that, and it is a big concession to make, many of the plays of this time packed a punch and had something to say. That they were trapped within the realistic form, the three-act, well-made play conventional to the point of predictability, was however a major disadvantage. Some writers of real talent, for example Walter Macken, Gerard Healy, Maurice Meldon, strained at the confines of realism, Macken bursting to get something new and raw said in *Mungo's Mansion* (1946) and especially in *Home is the Hero* (1952), but each time yielding to the taste of the day for melodrama and sensationalism. These two last-mentioned plays were about the lives of the poor in the tenements of Galway. *Home is the Hero* is about a violent man, Paddo Dowd, who is imprisoned for killing a man in a brawl and who on his release is unable to cope with his confusing reception as 'hero' and resorts to violence once again. In these plays Macken was too indebted to O'Casey's *Juno*. His most interesting play, though it lacks real action, was *Twilight of a Warrior* (1955), which queries the values of those whose sacrifice created modern Ireland. When the old warrior dies in his armchair in something close to despair the old Ireland seems to die with him.

On the other hand, Gerard Healy and Maurice

Meldon, as if recognising the suffocating atmosphere, left the Abbey and for all too brief a date did experimental work elsewhere in Dublin.[6] This left the Abbey stage to a few other stalwarts, George Shiels, Joseph Tomelty, Frank Carney and Louis D'Alton among them, names now probably no more than names, their plays well forgotten. And yet, to return to my theme, these people wrote plays that while firmly of their own time generate ideas we can still debate today, though quite differently.

George Shiels, who had been a 1920s favourite for his amusing if sentimental comedies, *Professor Tim* and *Paul Twying* among them, suddenly emerged as the harsh voice of the 1940s, of the war years, of the commemoration of the Great Famine (in *Tenants at Will*, 1945) and of a society painfully coming to terms with its moral deficiencies. A northerner, a man disabled by a horrific accident incurred in his youth in Canada, Shiels had an independent and unique point of view on modern Irish society. In 1940 his new play *The Rugged Path* was so successful he had to write a sequel, *The Summit*. Here was a major departure from his earlier comic material, although *The New Gossoon* (1930) and especially *The Passing Day* (1936) had shown that for all his ability to create comic characters and present a light-hearted view of life Shiels was awake to the changes overtaking the Irish state. His focus in *The Rugged Path* was on the crisis facing this new state with one foot in the past, in outmoded notions of loyalty to the clan rather than to the law of the land. Here Shiels seems to pick up on something Seán O Faoláin was saying at the time in *The Bell*:

> This struggle between the inescapable Past and the insistent Present, between luxuriating into nostalgia and working out of ambition, has

made itself felt strongly since 1916. If there is any distinct cleavage among us to-day it is between those who feel that tradition can explain everything, and those who think it can explain nothing … We are living … to a great extent experimentally, and must go on doing so.[7]

In Shiels's play Seán Tansey, son of a small farmer, is described as 'born free', the first man in his family history 'that never touched his cap to an alien'.[8] It wasn't just this, the growing pains of a people liberated from foreign domination; there was also the legacy of lawlessness or what the Garda Sergeant calls 'the national kink' of unwillingness to co-operate with the police: in short, the fear of being branded an informer (p. 21). Thus when a murder is committed and everyone in the district knows who did it, namely a family from the mountains called the Dolises, people are reluctant as well as afraid to give evidence. The Dolises are violent, lawless men but they are, so to speak, 'our own'; besides they terrorise the neighbourhood and it would be dangerous to report seeing or hearing anything which would incriminate them. Seán Tansey, standing for the new generation, argues for speaking out and manages to convince his father to give witness against the Dolises, for as Michael Tansey puts it: 'I wonder to God what decent men fought and died for! Was it for a country where a jury is afraid to bring in a verdict, and an old-age pensioner isn't allowed to live and die in peace!' (pp. 94–95). Shiels's point is that there cannot be a new Ireland until people change and accept responsibility for its moral condition. Yet even when Michael gives evidence the jury fails to convict the Dolises and the first play ends with the Tansey house under attack in reprisal. The second play is a test of nerve for the Tanseys and other people in the neighbourhood convinced likewise that a stand must be taken. The complication is that Cassidy, the neighbour who eventually sides with the Tanseys, is an old political enemy, another legacy from the civil war days. And when the showdown begins with the Dolises the threatened solution opens up more than one paradox in the search for justice:

CASSIDY: Now Dolis, I want to talk to you about [your son] Johnny. You won't be seeing him again for some time.
DOLIS: Where is he?
CASSIDY: He's in the barracks, I took him there myself in the car. And from there he'll be sent to a reformatory – or I'll know the reason why. I'll want to know what the hell a reformatory is for if not for Johnny Dolis ...
DOLIS: I couldn't stop him.
CASSIDY: Well, he's stopped now. Five or six years in an industrial school'll either kill him or cure him. You've done *your* part for him and [your other son] Peter.
DOLIS: I don't want a sermon, Cassidy!
CASSIDY: This is no sermon. I'm not so damned green as to start preaching to Hugh Dolis. I'm only telling you this racket has got to stop.
(p. 233)

Nowadays we can see the new legacy of cruelty and crime Cassidy's solution here promises. The industrial school was to prove a cure too far and the source of more problems than anyone in 1941 could, presumably, imagine and Cassidy's phrase, 'either kill or cure', is decidedly ominous. Thus the play in its confrontation with rural violence projects forward to our own day in more ways than one, principally, of course, in its focusing on the roots of violence and lawlessness in a colonialist tradition of resistance.

Shiels's two interconnected plays, *The Rugged Path* and *The Summit*, which are really one long play on an urgent theme, were enormously popular but not quite so popular as *The Righteous Are Bold* (1946) by Frank Carney, which ran for six months during its Abbey première. On one level this is good, old-fashioned melodrama involving the eternal battle between good and evil in the new shape of priest against demonic possession. Audiences loved the spectacle of the possessed girl rampaging around the Abbey stage blaspheming and spitting at a holy statue which she then dashed to bits on the tiny stage. Some solemn members of the audience would tot up the cost of the production via so many statues smashed per week over the long run; others shook in their shoes as the blasphemies hurtled across the tiny stage. But on another level the subtle propaganda of the piece related to Ireland's emergence from neutrality in World War II to look with deep suspicion on the moral dangers inherent in emigration by the young to England in search of employment. Nora Geraty, the young woman possessed, has just returned from England, where she had fallen among spiritualists, become a medium and in short become as it were infected with evil ideas. The home she returns to is a frugal homestead straight out of de Valera's hymn to the ideal Ireland; it is even located on the slopes of the holy mountain, Croagh Patrick. When Nora starts into her demonic routine she decries the Catholic church and its restraints and speaks for freedom and other such dangerous notions. Her mother and father, simple folk that they are, call upon a local witch-doctor figure, Nellie the Post, to work a charm to help their daughter in the traditional manner. But the priest who arrives to perform exorcism in the little cottage drives Nellie out with the cry to the Geratys, 'Haven't I enough to contend with without this pagan nonsense. I ask you to have faith and you turn to superstition. Must I be alone in the fight?'[9] Nora's brother, representing the younger generation once more, sides with her against the priest and brings their father round to this position, but the good Fr O'Malley, described in the text as 'a walking saint' (p. 41), easily shows that this display of intellectual independence is the fruit of Nora's demons at work in the household. To save her and the family and indeed the whole of Irish society she must be exorcised, in the major spectacular scene in the play.[10] That it costs the good Fr O'Malley his life in the struggle is no great matter as the play comes to a happy ending with the young Nora, freed from her demons at last, walking out hand-in-hand with her lover on the slopes of Croagh Patrick in the sunshine, miraculously restored.

The real struggle in this play is once again between tradition and modernity, but this time, in contrast to what was shown by Shiels, the major anxiety is not law and order but the religious beliefs of the people. The play shows how it is only through the dedication of the Catholic clergy that the people can remain safe from perdition. Thus were problems 'combed out' and 'rendered innocuous', that is, ironed out into orthodox views, on the Abbey stage. This play was to establish itself in the amateur drama movement as a major expression of 1950s Ireland until John B. Keane came along with a different, more sociologically based analysis of rural Ireland in *Sive* (1959) and its successors.

Viewed in revival as late as1988 *The Righteous Are Bold*

could still be regarded by the *Irish Times* critic as 'a fascinating social document of an Irish society that is far from disappearing'.[11] Today, sixteen years on, all is changed utterly and the church no longer maintains its 'moral monopoly' upon the minds and choices of the people.[12] Yet even so does not the question remain, 'where are the demons now?' How do we define them or do we simply dismiss them along with MacLíammóir's mythic revenants? In abandoning tradition for modernity have we thrown out the real baby with the superstitious bathwater?

One could and perhaps should say something here also about the plays of M.J. Molloy, which were popular in the 1950s and for longer among amateur drama groups. Molloy wrote poetically, plangently and colourfully about rural life and customs in the west of Ireland. Essentially, he wrote about an Ireland that was even then passing. Unlike Shiels, Molloy lamented the passing of the old folk ways and the old, unquestioning religious outlook. His plays, whether the historical *King of Friday's Men* (1948) or the contemporary *Wood of the Whispering* (1953), were even in their day elegies for a lost community; today they are museum pieces, beautiful curiosities eloquent of a culture and a people so remote from us that we cannot find a response beyond puzzlement and a shameful kind of laughter. They have had no discernible impact on late twentieth century Irish drama. It is startling to think that as late as 1979 Molloy had a new play staged at the Abbey, *Petticoat Loose*, one more folk drama, set in nineteenth century Ireland. That door is firmly closed now against revenants.

A final example here of the drama of this period is Louis D'Alton's *This Other Eden*. D'Alton, who had his own touring company, was a man who knew the theatre inside out. Many of his plays were either strong melodramas or satirical comedies; he did not, like O'Casey, dare to combine the two. He was a lesser artist and yet a good one. *This Other Eden* is his best play. It held the record for the longest run in the history of the Abbey, twenty-six weeks. The much-lamented Séamus De Búrca, in a letter to *The Irish Times* in 1994, puzzled over the Abbey's failure to revive this play, D'Alton's 'masterpiece'.[13] Over ten years on, even in the year of the Abbey's celebratory centenary De Búrca's appeal has not been heard. This is strange, given the pointed social commentary of *This Other Eden*. For while D'Alton dealt once more with the complacencies of post-war Ireland and showed a society subdued by clerical domination, he was far too independent a writer to hew to the conventional lines of Abbey plot-making.

Set in 1947 *This Other Eden* concerns the commemoration in a small town of a native civil-war hero whose heroism masks a secret which is covered up by church-state hypocrisy. Tradition is held up to severe and satirical scrutiny. More forcefully than in any Abbey play of its time the younger generation expresses disillusion with Ireland's warped idealism, which we hear Máire McRoarty, the daughter of one of the town's big businessmen, dare to attack as she states her preference for a life in England. In striking contrast to Nora Geraty in *The Righteous Are Bold* D'Alton's Máire is far from being possessed or perceived as such. She is a level-headed, sensible, independent woman who wants to leave Ireland principally because, as she puts it, 'I like the feeling that I can go to the devil in my own way if I feel like doing that. And because I don't like the feeling that I must go to heaven someone else's way whether I like it or not. And because I like the feeling of being able to talk to a man, or even half a dozen men, without being suspected of wanting to go to bed with them!'[14] There are other dissident voices in the play also, and the illegitimate son of the war hero burns down the memorial hall erected for his father as a gesture of rejection. There is in addition an English eccentric, Roger Crispin, who like a figure from Shaw, notably *John Bull's Other Island*, sets everybody's thoughts in a spin by his cool refusal to accept the orthodoxies held fast by the local priest and politician. Add a cynical and articulate schoolteacher, Devereaux, and the cross-section of mid-century Irish provinciality is complete. Devereaux is described as 'a man of first-class ability whose life has been wasted in a backwater ... The bitterness of a man who has witnessed, as he believes, his country fall from grace, and the disappointment of his own hopes is always with him' (p. 6). From this mix we get a sense of intelligence struggling to bend back the iron bars which hold the new generation prisoner. The play came like a breath of fresh air at the Queen's Theatre (Pearse Street) in 1953, where the Abbey company had moved after the 1951 fire. Unfortunately, D'Alton was by then dead at the early age of fifty-one and a considerable career in the Irish theatre was cut short. But already he had pointed the way forward for those new playwrights who would continue to revolt against the stifling atmosphere of post-war Ireland, in particular Friel, Leonard, Keane, Kilroy and Murphy.

There were few works at the time which dared go against Blythe's homely vision of an Ireland where all problems could be solved over a cup of tea. One exception would be Seamus Byrne's *Design for a Headstone* (1950), a play set in Mountjoy jail concerning IRA prisoners on hunger-strike for political status: this caused a furore because of its outspokenness. It is a prime example of the kind of play outshone by its successors, notably Behan's *The Quare Fellow* (1954), staged at the newly formed Pike Theatre, founded for the very reason that Behan's work and its like had no place on the Abbey stage. D'Alton's *This Other Eden* was another exception, a play ahead of its time, a play which paved the way for the likes of Murphy's *Conversations on a Homecoming* (1985). It was filmed in 1959 just as the old Ireland was yielding to the new under Seán Lemass. As Fidelma Farley, author of a recent little book on this landmark achievement, has remarked: 'the film [of *This Other Eden*] marks a new beginning, however tentative, of the critical exploration of Irish society and national identity that would characterize Irish cinema from the 1970s to the present'.[15]

To return to MacLíammóir, by way of conclusion, in his short study of Irish drama MacLíammóir referred to 'the fatal fifties' in Ireland.[16] There was stagnation in the theatre as in society at this time. Is there literally such a thing as energy in society which runs low in some decades and revives in others? It would seem so. The inevitable happy ending which was *de rigueur* in most Irish plays at this period betokens a loss of energy as well as a loss of critical intelligence. The question as applied to the playwrights of the 1940s and 1950s, 'where are they now?', has two possible answers. One is the obvious one, that most are forgotten in the merciless way in which time sifts and dismisses past achievements. Time's wallet is pretty stuffed with the best intentions of the Abbey at mid-century.[17] But there is another, more positive answer. These writers, or at least the handful whose voices were individual enough to pierce through the muffled conventionalities of the day, are all around us like ghosts. Writers who strike a chord in their own day, who hit upon a contemporary mood or obsession, set up echoes for later generations to hear, however faintly, in others.

When a reviewer of *This Other Eden* said in 1953 that, 'Our playwrights are to-day's ballad-makers,'[18] he meant that they were articulating feelings and stories which resonated with audiences. We might be more inclined to say they were struggling to define the audience's location between tradition and modernity. Our balladeers, having undergone the influence of protest songs from abroad in the 1960s, sing a different tune today. If the 'ballads' of the 1940s and 1950s are heard at all nowadays it is as echoes in the work of altogether different writers reworking this major preoccupation in new accents, new rhythms and a new vocabulary which would doubtless have terrified their almost-forgotten forebears.

NOTES

[1] See Peter Kavanagh, *The Story of the Abbey Theatre* (New York: Devin-Adair, 1950), p.184.

[2] The most commonly cited evidence of a collapse of artistic standards is the so-called 'Abbey Incident' in November 1947, when a controversy grew up around a protest at a bad performance of *The Plough and the Stars*. See Hugh Hunt, *The Abbey: Ireland's National Theatre 1904–1979* (Dublin: Gill and Macmillan, 1979), pp. 173–74.

[3] Micheál MacLíammóir, Preface, *Where Stars Walk: A Fantasy* (Dublin: Progress House, 1962), n.p., emphasis added.

[4] Cited by Gabriel Fallon, *Irish Monthly*, LXVIII (1940), p. 561.

[5] Ernest Blythe, *The Abbey Theatre* (Dublin: National Theatre Society Ltd, n.d.), n.p. The preceding quotation is from the same source.

[6] The actor Gerard Healy, whose *Thy Dear Father* was staged at the Abbey in 1943, left to found the Players' Theatre, for which he wrote a good play on the Famine, *The Black Stranger* (1945). Maurice Meldon's *House under Green Shadows* was staged at the Abbey in 1951; he then left for the 37 Theatre Club, for which his satiric fantasy *Aisling*, directed by Barry Cassin, had a resounding success in 1953. Similarly, Donagh MacDonagh's poetic extravaganza *Happy as Larry* could get only a brief showing in 1947. It later won fame in London and New York.

[7] Seán O Faoláin, '1916–1941: Tradition and Creation', *The Bell*, 2 (April 1941), p. 6.

[8] George Shiels, *The Rugged Path & The Summit: Plays in Three Acts* (London: Macmillan, 1942), p. 92. Subsequent quotations refer to this text and will be given by page numbers in parentheses.

[9] Frank Carney, *The Righteous Are Bold: A Play in Three Acts* (Dublin: James Duffy, 1951), p. 61.

[10] Although he did not see this play, Seán O'Casey heard about it and read the reviews and was so amused that he parodied the exorcism scene in *Cock-a-Doodle Dandy* (1949).

[11] David Nowlan, '*The Righteous Are Bold* at the Olympia', *The Irish Times*, 26 August 1988.

[12] See Tom Inglis, *Moral Monopoly: The Rise and Fall of the Catholic Church in Modern Ireland* (Dublin: UCD Press, 1998).

[13] Séamus De Búrca to *The Irish Times*, 8 October 1994.

[14] Louis D'Alton, *This Other Eden: A Play in Three Acts*, 2nd edition (Dublin: P.J. Bourke, 1970), p. 70.

[15] Fidelma Murphy, *Ireland into Film: This Other Eden* (Cork: Cork University Press, in association with the Film Institute of Ireland, 2001), p. 83. See also Ciara O'Farrell, *A Playwright's Journey: A Critical Biography of Louis D'Alton* (Dublin: TownHouse, 2004).

[16] Micheál MacLíammóir, *Theatre in Ireland*, 2nd edition (Dublin: Cultural Relations Committee of Ireland, 1964), p. 57.

[17] Cf. William Shakespeare, *Troilus and Cressida*, ed. Kenneth Palmer, Arden Shakespeare (London: Methuen, 1982), 3.3.146–47.

[18] Gabriel Fallon, *Standard*, 12 June 1953.

A SCENE FROM THE FIRST PRODUCTION OF *AT
THE BLACK PIG'S DYKE* BY VINCENT WOODS,
DIRECTED BY MAELÍOSA STAFFORD AND
DESIGNED BY MONICA FRAWLEY. DRUID
THEATRE COMPANY, 1992.

Druid Theatre Archive. Photo: Amelia Stein.

LYNDA HENDERSON

THEATRE BEYOND THE
BLACK PIG'S DYKE:
ULSTER DRAMA

'Theatre in Ulster' involves two things –
'theatre' and 'Ulster' – generally demonstrating little interest in each other. But
when theatre and its society communicate,
they can generate real change.

Ulster has always been a place apart.
It lies behind natural defences of
drumlins, water, forests and the pre-
historic earthworks of the Black Pig's
Dyke – a sort of Irish Hadrian's Wall.
The seventeenth century plantations reinforced this separateness.

The volume of planters and the
massive building programme of twenty-
three new towns to house them testify that
the Ulster plantations were designed to
succeed. They bred a people consciously
existing in a state of permanent siege,
driven by three key imperatives:

- to dig in where they were

- to stay apart from the native Irish
- to prosper

To dig in, to stay apart, to prosper – when these govern your very existence, there's little room for the life of the imagination, which is playful, inclusive, time-wasting, fantastic, impractical and unguarded. Indeed, for the imagination, 'otherness' is to be explored, not resisted. Moreover, digging in, staying apart and prospering are, by their absolute focus on the mundane and on the here and now, inimical to the imaginative process.

The Ulster planters have had neither the leisure nor the cultural equipment to engage much with the imagination.

So you have a Catholic minority whose sustained sense of displacement finds its outlet in the poetry of lament that shivers the heartstrings of Irish émigrés the world over. And you have those newly possessed: busy, hard-working, organised, driven, defensive – and resented. Their loss is just as enduring but remains unrecognised, even by themselves – an effective disbarment from the life of the spirit, leaving their experiences unformed, uninterrogated and unsung.

Now, agreed, there's nothing less attractive than an Ulster Protestant in full 'not an inch' fig. But – how few people have stopped to weigh the cultural impact of knowing oneself to be universally disliked?

Ulster, of course, remains unreconciled – internally and externally. But its theatre has persistently, if sporadically, laboured towards resolution.

- It has been consciously used to evolve a
  sense of inclusive nationhood.
- It has described the nature of contemporary
  life in the province.

- It has explored the cultural impact of violence.
- It has revealed the majority Protestant culture to itself and others.

From the beginning of the twentieth century, theatre in Ulster was an instrument of integration and, with the theatre in Dublin, was part of a European revolution in theatre itself. Suddenly, from large auditoriums, two dimensional scenic backdrops and 'big' acting, a more intimate theatre emerged, playing in smaller spaces to fewer people.

Stage settings became three dimensional and realistic, looking like rooms people knew in their own lives. Actors started talking to each other, moving about the stage as if in a real room, even turning their backs on the audience, refusing to recognise their presence. Plots became naturalistic, events being seen to spring from a cause the audience could identify. Ordinary lives were accepted as fit subjects for drama. All of this made it easier for theatre to enter into a dialogue with its audiences. In Ireland at the turn of the twentieth century, still under British rule, theatre was keen to do this and it had plenty to talk about.

Yeats's Irish Literary Theatre staged its first productions in Dublin in 1899. These soon set a pattern of presenting plays with a contemporary political theme alongside those with a nostalgic take on nationalism through reviving legend and folklore.

In 1902, in Belfast, two young Protestants, Bulmer Hobson and David Parkhill, who had been trying — without much success — to promote the ideas of Wolfe Tone and the United Irishmen, wondered if drama might be a productive medium. They decided to create an Ulster Branch of the Irish Literary Theatre and set off on the train to Dublin to get Yeats's support.

Yeats gave them the elbow – they said he was 'haughty and aloof'. So their modest wish for a junior partnership in a national movement had to translate into a sort of theatrical UDI. Hobson and Parkhill had to go it alone. They set up the Ulster Literary Theatre, the ULT.

The next few years saw very real successes, with acclamation for tours to Dublin and London. And Yeats himself said of their first visit to Dublin in 1907:

> the absence of the ordinary conventions, the novelty of movement and intonation ... The Ulster Players are the only dramatic society, apart from our own, which is doing serious artistic work.

In 1905 David Parkhill's play *The Enthusiast* (written as Lewis Purcell) proposed the value of collective farming. James, the enthusiast, is unable to overcome his Antrim farming family's resistance to the idea. They are too fearful of 'home rulers', Catholics and fenians. So he goes for a mass local meeting to publicise the proposals more widely – but holds it in his family's biggest field instead of in the Orange Hall. Unfortunately this guarantees that sectarian suspicion on the Protestant side will sabotage consideration of the idea and his attempt ends in failure.

Parkhill was probably influenced by Sir Horace Plunkett's Irish Agricultural Organisation, founded in 1901. This made such an impact in Ulster farming circles that *The Enthusiast* was revived in 1909. As Thomas Davis would have appreciated, the major success of this play was showing the contemporary Ulsterman to himself for the first time. The writer Cathal O'Shannon, in the audience for the tour of *The Enthusiast* to Toome Bridge in 1905, wrote:

> for the first time I saw that the kind of people

that I knew and lived among in Co Antrim and
Co Derry were there, alive and talking as they
talked at home.

James Connolly had suggested that the Ulster Literary
Theatre should 'attempt to realise Ulster to the rest of
Ireland'. The ULT's strategy was to achieve this by first
working to realise Ulster to itself. They had three main
achievements.

- They cast Ulster actors in their plays, creating
  an immediate cultural familiarity in the community on both sides of the curtain.
- They wrote dialogue that reflected current
  Ulster speech.
- They staged plays that invited their audiences
  to enter into a debate on the progressive issues
  of the day.

The ULT continued – as The Ulster Theatre – until after
1940, when it became the foundation for the Ulster
Group Theatre. The Group Theatre carried the standard
of the ULT in producing, in 1958, Gerard McLarnon's
play *The Bonefire*. You get some insights into its courageous
and provocative subject matter from the response of a
contemporary critic:

It is a vomit of disgust. A foreigner seeing this
presentation by the Ulster Group Theatre at
the Edinburgh Festival next month will not
react to it as would an Ulster Catholic or an
Ulster Protestant. He will not see that the
Orange bigots and the spineless Catholics on
the stage are crude caricatures.

Then there was the controversy surrounding Sam
Thomson's play *Over the Bridge*, eventually produced in

1960 at Belfast's Empire Theatre. This exposed a rampant sectarianism in the shipyards of Belfast and its production was long suppressed by the Protestant establishment. Indeed the Ulster Group Theatre itself withdrew from producing it.

Over the years a succession of plays continued the 'realisation of Ulster' to itself and to the world beyond. John Boyd's 1971 play, *The Flats*, showed the impact of violence on the communities in the infamous high-rise flats in the Belfast of the time. Graham Reid's 1982 play, *The Hidden Curriculum*, presented with realism and humour the extent to which violence as a means to an end enters the repertoire of the young. Martin Lynch's 1982 play, *The Interrogation of Ambrose Fogarty*, pointed up the innocent victims of a state with an uncertain grasp of the nature of democracy.

There were plays recording the invisible lives of the working classes, ground down by sectarianism and capitalism. In 1981 there was Martin Lynch's *Dockers*, in 1982 Frank McGuinness's *Factory Girls* – about workers in the Derry shirt-making industry – and 1983 saw the Charabanc Theatre Company's *Lay Up Your Ends*, celebrating the lives of the women workers in the linen mills at the time of the Connolly strike in 1911.

Charabanc's second play, *Oul Delf and False Teeth*, featured the women stall-holders of Belfast's Smithfield Market during the 1945 post-war election. Peter Mandelson would recognise the skill of the Unionist government of the day in stilling the threat of Ireland's only real labour movement. It played the Orange card – arousing Protestant insecurity by linking labour to Irish nationalism – and won. This play carried the sharpest political statement of Charabanc's many plays. Bertha, the most bigoted character and a paid-up party member, goes to the Unionist leader Carson's rally at the Ulster Hall. There she discovers that her place is with her working-class peers outside the wire fences where they can hear but not see – and certainly not touch – the great man. She offers her savings to secure a seat inside. But not even money can bridge the gap dividing her from her middle-class Unionist brethren – a painful revelation.

The impact of theatre companies on life in Ulster has been pretty mixed. The Lyric Players Theatre was founded in 1951 by Mary and Pearse O'Malley in their home in Belfast, later housed in a purpose-built theatre by the River Lagan. It was committed to poetic drama and particularly to Yeats. Energetic as this was, it came to blind the Lyric to its immediate circumstances – which were becoming increasingly dramatic and politically urgent. This out-of-touch-ness was most evident in 1968 and after – the time of Europe-wide student protest – when theatre was to be found more on the streets of Ulster than on its stages.

During a long night on the 1969 march from Belfast to Derry of the young People's Democracy movement – with a brutal Paisleyite ambush at Burntollett Bridge – Bernadette Devlin records the fun of an impromptu theatrical event. The students – Catholic and Protestant – who were the core of the People's Democracy were waiting for an enforced police escort around Randalstown. They passed the time by enacting the imaginary trial of RUC County Inspector Cramsie, who particularly got up their noses. Devlin records:

> Fergus Woods was the only one among us
> charitable enough to be counsel for the defence
> and the plea he made was on the grounds of

insanity. His evidence was Cramsie's hat, a sort of Scots piper's forage cap perched on the side of the head, which Fergus said no sane man would wear. Counsel for the prosecution said the hat was, on the contrary, further damning evidence of incompetence, because it was a model for *cadet* County Inspectors only. Cramsie was found guilty and sentenced to becoming caretaker of Eton playing fields in perpetuity. We all enjoyed watching the policemen in the cordon trying to keep straight faces and Cramsie getting more outraged by the minute and inviting us to 'grow up'.

Shortly afterwards, in the same year, Britain and Ireland were electrified by other pieces of popular theatre. There was the fluent, extempore and passionate maiden speech in Westminster of the young, long-haired, mini-skirted Bernadette Devlin, newly elected as MP for South Derry. And there were, shortly, press photos of the same MP hurling a brick from a barricade.

It's hard to believe now, but while this was the theatre of life at the time, Belfast's Lyric Theatre was presenting plays from the classical and folk repertoire. It was producing nothing then that in any way reflected or approached the vitality of the current events that looked likely to change the bipartisan nature of Ulster society.

Another theatrical foundation that promised to contribute to the relationship between Ulster and the rest of Ireland was the Field Day Theatre Company. This was established in 1980 in Derry by the writer-and-actor partnership of Brian Friel and Stephen Rea.

Its first production, Friel's play *Translations*, was an immediate international success. Underlining the double abuse of an occupied country with the cultural suffocation of the native language, it went on to become widely translated itself as the touchstone for the condition everywhere of the dispossessed. This stellar impact secured the authority of the company's voice.

The productions and publications undertaken by Field Day amount to serious and valuable cultural analysis and commentary. The company could, though, be said to have dropped the theatrical ball on two major scoring opportunities. It was offered Frank McGuinness's play *Observe the Sons of Ulster Marching towards the Somme* — and rejected it. Fortunately the Abbey Theatre in Dublin simultaneously recognised the play's worth, producing it in 1985. Field Day went on to commission a play from David Rudkin, also exploring the Ulster Protestant culture. This was intended as a counterpoint to the nationalist focus of their first production, *Translations*. But the company declined to produce the resulting play, *The Saxon Shore*. Although quickly staged in London, it has never received a professional production in Ireland. These are two powerful plays that, with four others, arguably have the most to say in Ulster's more recent self-examination.

Stewart Parker's *Northern Star* centres on Henry Joy McCracken, the Protestant leader of the United Irishmen's Ulster action in their failed 1798 Rebellion against British rule. In a complex poetic play McCracken is seen waiting for execution. Desperate in his awareness that 'we botched the birth' of a united Ireland, he finally expresses his profound yet unblinkered love of Ulster:

> Why would one place break your heart, more than another? A place the like of that? Brain-damaged and dangerous, continually violating

itself, a place of perpetual breakdown, incompatible voices, screeching obscenely away through the smoky dark wet. Burnt out and still burning. Nerve-damaged, pitiable. Frightening.

1984 also saw the publication in *Theatre Ireland* of a play from a very unexpected source – the Ulster Defence Association, the main Protestant paramilitary organisation. The play was co-written by its leader, Andy Tyrie, with Sam Duddy, a folk poet and member of the UDA's Council, and Michael Hall, a pacifist employee of the National Society for the Prevention of Cruelty to Children.

The UDA and the Provisional IRA were in regular contact through trusted intermediaries and were discovering that their current political thinking was remarkably similar. Each wanted an Ulster free of British rule. Each was evolving proposals for replacing the Stormont government with a system of community politics. Each was prepared to share Ulster with the other. The play was written to carry this debate to the UDA's grassroots through planned productions in Protestant working-men's clubs. Tyrie hoped that it might eventually play in Republican working-men's clubs and that they might 'send us back a play'. Now there's an awareness of the role of art in life.

The play expressed a strong anti-Paisleyite position, a love of Ulster, a fear of suffering the fate of the Palestinians in being driven from their homeland and, therefore, a readiness to share with those previously seen as enemies. The title, *This Is It*, underlined the urgency of the choice to be made.

The next year – 1985 – saw the Abbey Theatre's production of McGuinness's *Observe the Sons of Ulster Marching towards the Somme*. In an act of unparalleled cultural courage and generosity, McGuinness, a Catholic from County Donegal, set out to explore the nature of the people who shared his country. He found self-dislike and saw it as the foundation for a sort of death wish – a willingness to die for Ulster, perhaps to validate being there. The play's metaphor is the legendary status in Ulster Protestant culture of the Ulster Volunteer Force, annihilated at the battle of the Somme.

Four pairs of soldiers represent the various parts of Ulster. All are Protestant though one, secretly, is from a mixed marriage. The competitiveness, the camaraderie and the pressures of battle test their prejudices to destruction. What is left is love of place and the play ends with them, on the eve of death, chanting repeatedly the word 'Ulster'.

1986 saw the London production of Rudkin's *The Saxon Shore*. It translates the Ulster Protestants into a Saxon tribe planted by the Romans below Hadrian's Wall to keep down the Picts. Surviving alone in that comfortless place for generations their successive identities give place to the feral. At nightfall they become werewolves, crossing the wall to savage and kill their given enemies. On one raid, Athdark, their leader, is wounded. He wakes to find himself in paradise. There is light, music, dance, gaiety and an enchanting girl. Slowly he realises he is in the hands of the enemy – and learns to think for himself. But Rome hits trouble back home and the border garrisons in northern Britain are recalled. The Saxon tribe are left without defence, facing a numerically superior enemy with every reason to destroy them. The parson's wife, Agnes, speaks for the tribe and for today's Ulster Protestants in denouncing the empire which has used them as pawns in its own game:

Well for you, Imperial mighty Power! Set us

and native British at each others' throats; now forsake us naked to their rage. And have the gall to preach at us! Covenant, you call this? Take everything away from a folk? Land? Roots? All our belongings? Pluck us up and plant us in this foreign island where we have no belonging? Where we must rob and savage to thrive at all? Then give us no defence? Covenant? Not even a name. British, and not. Saxon, and not. Roman, and not. Who shall we say that we are now?

In 1994 Marie Jones's international success with *A Night in November* centres on a bigoted Protestant dole clerk, taking every opportunity his job offers him to deny and humiliate Catholic claimants. The first dint in his armour is his private shame at joining in the dreadful sectarian chanting at the international football match in Belfast between Northern Ireland and the Republic of Ireland. 'Greysteel 7, Ireland Nil' celebrated a recent random assassination of seven Catholics in a small village pub in County Derry.

Later, uncharacteristically, he gives a lift home to a Catholic colleague and runs into a domestic chaos he recognises as demonstrating a different set of cultural values. Here are toys that are used, books that are read, games that are played. Finally he deceives his wife and sneaks off to Dublin. He joins the thousands of supporters flying out to New York to support Jack Charlton's Republic of Ireland team in its World Cup quarter final.

At Dublin airport he is automatically welcome as a fellow fan. He's lent a supporters' T-shirt, given contacts in New York who will put him up and brought to an Irish pub to watch the match with his new-found friends. For the first time in his life he feels acceptance, fellowship, inclusion, a sense of belonging. He has supported Ireland. He has been hugged by other men. Nothing will be the same again. The play ends with his words:

> I am free of it. I am a free man. I am a Protestant man. I'm an Irish man.

So the Catholic McGuinness began a cultural reaching out with his sensitive exploration of the Protestant psyche. This process continued in Rudkin's and Jones's interrogation of that culture from within – and in their romantic presentation of the nationalist culture. The generous evaluation of the other is a necessary stage in the rapprochement that must eventually come.

Building on these advances has been Gary Mitchell's resolute self-alignment with his own culture, married to a willingness to scrutinise its most sacred cows. In *The Force of Change*, produced in 2000, he presented a critique from inside the Protestant culture of the organisation with which nationalists most closely associate it – the Royal Ulster Constabulary. He shows it as being tainted with sexism, guilty of collusion with Protestant paramilitary forces – yet prepared to offer violence to anyone, Protestant or Catholic, friend or foe, who might obstruct it. He offers no bland conclusions or prescriptions.

Together, these six plays contribute to and chart change in Ulster – change yet to reach fruition but significant nevertheless.

You can tell a thousand stories from the same body of material. This is only one.

There are other stories that could be told – such as the contribution of Ulster theatre to the evolution of theatre

throughout the island, which has been considerable.
There are other stories that should be told – the story of
those in the 'lost' Ulster counties of Donegal, Cavan and
Monaghan; and more of the Ulster Catholic's experience
of life under Protestant majority rule.

But what would please Thomas Davis, Protestant
leader of the Young Ireland movement, is that twentieth
century theatre beyond the Black Pig's Dyke has played its
part in the fulfilment of his key concerns:

- to acquire knowledge of our present cultures
- to evolve a sense of nationhood capable of
  including us all

RAY MCANALLY AND GERARD MCSORLEY IN
THE 1982 ABBEY THEATRE PRODUCTION OF
BRIAN FRIEL'S *PHILADELPHIA, HERE I COME!*,
DIRECTED BY JOE DOWLING AND
DESIGNED BY FRANK CONWAY.

Abbey National Theatre Archives. Photo: Fergus Bourke.

JOE DOWLING

A VIEW FROM THE MISSISSIPPI

Looking out my window in downtown Minneapolis, Minnesota, the mighty Mississippi flows past, determined to take all before it on its long journey to the sea. It is a spectacle that both inspires and intimidates – it promises new excitements to the traveller but it can also lead to dangerous and unknown shores. The river as metaphor is a tired device but when I think back on thirty-five years in the professional theatre, I cannot help seeing it as both a literal and figurative journey. My love affair with theatre started as a young boy growing up in Dublin in the fifties and the passion remains undimmed to this day. Ireland was a very different place in those pre-Whitaker, pre-Lemass Programme for Economic Expansion years, where opportunities were limited, expectations

low and the only tigers around were up in the zoo.
Without any family history in the arts, it seemed like an
exotic world well beyond my grasp. People like us did not
go into theatre. Where I came from, the expected career
path was to become a teacher, a civil servant or a
respectable member of other permanent and pensionable
professions. The tributary of professional theatre was
unknown and frightening territory. Even where one
should start to plan for such a career was a mystery.

A resourceful and determined grandmother, who may
have harboured such longings herself, enrolled me in a
drama class with the formidable but brilliant Ena Mary
Burke. It was in her musty studio at 20 Kildare Street that
a love of the spoken word was born and nurtured in me.
Shakespeare was Ena Burke's passion and she had a deep
understanding of how his great poetry should be spoken.
Year after year at the Father Maitiu feis her students
would sweep the boards and we began to think of
ourselves as stars in our own little firmament. Performing
on a stage was a sublime joy for me and, gradually, the
idea that it could be more than a hobby was planted in
my mind. As we listened to Burkie's tales of how she had
trained Maureen O'Hara, Milo O'Shea, Eamon Andrews
and others whose names were in lights, the idea of
becoming a part of that world seemed slightly less
impossible. It was still a far-off and unlikely destination
but at least the journey seemed less daunting.

I have indeed travelled a long way from my first
theatre-going experiences when, every year, we made a
family pilgrimage to the Gaiety Theatre to delight in the
Christmas pantomime. For a star-struck child growing up
in Dublin in the late fifties, there was no greater treat than
that annual visit. From September on, I longed for the
shortening of the days and the onset of winter weather

that would bring the special day nearer. Giddy with anticipation and expectation on the bus journey, arriving at the theatre and mingling with the audience was a special part of the experience. Before the curtain rose, the sound of the orchestra tuning up and the smell of the size used in painting the sets were enough of a heady combination to induce near nirvana.

Even at a remove of nearly half a century, I can still experience the excitement and the breath-taking delight I felt at the sight of Jimmy O'Dea and Maureen Potter arriving in splendid style to oversee our journey into a land of fairy-tale magic where good always triumphed over bad, where dames were invariably men and girls were always principal boys. That pantomime has survived both the television and the Internet age is a remarkable testament to its enduring freshness and to the power of live theatre to engage the juvenile imagination.

Nowadays, it is common for performers from television to honour the theatre with a once-a-year performance in the annual pantomime ritual. In the fifties and sixties, before the advent of the TV star, pantomime in Dublin had its own stars associated with rival theatres. Jimmy and Maureen at the Gaiety, Cecil Sheridan and Noel Purcell at the Theatre Royal and Jack Cruise at the Olympia battled it out for supremacy. Different camps were established. Loyalties were tested and rarely did anyone betray them. While I knew some deprived children who had to make do with the Olympia, I belonged body and soul to South King Street and to the magic of O'Dea and Potter. The recent death of Maureen Potter saddened all those who remembered her extraordinary career from child star, through variety and pantomime to a great period later in her life where she proved herself an actor of depth and stature. Maureen was a diminutive genius who presided over the Gaiety Theatre for many years and her sense of comic timing combined with a remarkable natural instinct made it possible for her to straddle the world of pantomime and 'legitimate' theatre. As I sat in the Gaiety stalls entranced by my first exposure to the magic of live theatre, I could never have imagined that, many years later, I would direct Maureen in a number of shows and become her friend.

The early sixties are generally regarded as fallow times for Irish theatre, with the Abbey in exile across the Liffey in the Queen's Theatre and Micheál MacLíammóir and Hilton Edwards a spent force at the Gate. Yet, in spite of this seeming malaise, two of the greatest experiences of my theatre-going life occurred in my teenage years. From an early age I had become an inveterate theatre-goer, using whatever pocket money I could muster to get the cheapest seats. I saw a great many bad productions and some gems. The two that stand out both involved the MacLíammóir/Edwards Company. Micheál MacLíammóir was a legendary figure in Dublin in those years. My mother remembered his Hamlet in the early thirties and talked of him as the greatest matinée idol of her time. However, those years were well behind him and, with the exception of a few outings in undistinguished productions, it looked as if he was a figure of the past.

Then came *The Importance of Being Oscar*, his one-man show celebrating the life and work of Oscar Wilde. With this show, directed and lit by his partner Hilton Edwards, he once again became the most outstanding Irish theatrical personality of his time and my young imagination was transfixed by his remarkable stage presence. MacLíammóir stood alone on the Gaiety stage with a set consisting of a chair, a circular carpet, a table with a floral arrangement and nothing else. Dressed in an impeccable evening suit with the inevitable green carnation in his lapel, he took us through the life and works of a writer whose reputation had not yet been fully restored. The whiff of scandal surrounding Oscar Wilde had endured for more than sixty years after his death and, while his literary reputation was fast being restored, his infamous trial and prosecution were still not discussed in most social circles.

MacLíammóir and Edwards confronted that controversy in a discreet way but with honesty and taste. The theatrical genius of MacLíammóir was how easily he created both male and female characters from Wilde's plays and poetry without any change of costume or, indeed, of voice. I can still hear his remarkably rich tones playing with the beauty of the language from Wilde's cry of pain from prison, *The Ballad of Reading Gaol*:

> With midnight always in one's heart,
> And Twilight in one's cell,
> We turn the crank, or tear the rope,
> Each in his separate Hell,
> And the silence is more awful far
> Than the sound of a brazen bell.

His rendering of *De Profundis* was delivered with tenderness and a compassion that brought tears for Oscar and his Bosie. His Lady Bracknell from *The Importance of Being Earnest* was comparable with the great Dame Edith Evans herself. The theatrical moment when the judge sentenced Oscar Wilde to prison still chills the blood with its cruel tones and the depth of intolerance.

Given the social attitudes and legal restrictions concerning homosexuality at the time, much of the work was coded, yet MacLíammóir came closer to an identification with Oscar Wilde than was probably wise in a world where the writ of Archbishop John Charles McQuaid ran so firmly and where the belt of a crozier had already brought many notable personages to their knees. He could not talk openly of his own sexuality but, even to my hazy adolescent awareness, there could be no doubt about where his sympathies lay. It was a brave performance and one that gave the genre of the one-person show a new lease of life. There were many imitators but none could match the genius and the simplicity of that show and I saw it as often as finances and the boring pressures of school would allow.

It has often struck me since then that Micheál and Hilton were unique figures in more than their great contributions to Irish theatre. Living an openly gay life in their famous Harcourt Terrace home, they defied the restrictive authority of Irish society and they conquered triumphantly. Their Gate Theatre was subsidised in the late sixties by a determined and enlightened Charles Haughey. They dined with presidents and, when the inevitable happened, they both received the closest thing to state funerals that a grateful republic could provide.

In the seventies, as a young actor and director, I met both of them and, indeed, these heroes did not have feet of clay. In an inspired piece of television programming, Louis Lentin, then a producer in RTÉ, paired Hilton Edwards and myself in a series of filmed conversations in 1978. It was just after Micheál's death. As the grand old man of Irish theatre, Hilton shared his insights and reminiscences with me, then just appointed as the youngest-ever artistic director of the Abbey Theatre. The conversations were fascinating. Hilton was expansive and generous about most areas of his life and his art. The one area he refused to talk about was the deep and abiding dispute with the late Lord Longford. It was Longford who had rescued the Gate from financial ruin in the thirties but a serious dispute saw the break-up of the partnership. Longford went on to create his own company and the split meant that the seasons at the Gate were divided between him and MacLíammóir/Edwards. It was not a happy arrangement. When Louis Lentin and I persisted in an attempt to get Hilton to talk about the rift, he declined with force, saying in that inimitable fruity voice, 'I have no intention of destroying a lifetime's discretion for one moment's frisson on television.'

Hilton Edwards was also part of my second great theatrical epiphany. When I first saw Brian Friel's *Philadelphia, Here I Come!* at the Gaiety in 1964, I knew my life had changed forever. Since childhood, I had been star struck and my teenage years had been spent in such palaces of delight as the Gate, the Eblana, the Lantern and, the tiniest of all, the Pocket Theatre in Ely Place. Brave pioneers such as Phyllis Ryan, Godfrey Quigley, Barry Cassin, Paddy and Patricia Funge and, of course, the legendary Micheál and Hilton all formed part of my pantheon of heroes.

Recently, in celebrating the twentieth anniversary of that notable theatre company Rough Magic, today's leading critic, Fintan O'Toole, announced solemnly in *The Irish Times* that, before Rough Magic was formed in the early eighties, no English plays were done in Dublin. Mr O'Toole ought to have done a little research. Godfrey Quigley's Globe Theatre Company, Phyllis Ryan and Norman Rodway's Gemini Productions and many other smaller companies were all mounting the plays of the day from our neighbouring island – and from the world beyond – before Fintan was born. In the sixties, we had Osborne in the Gate, Sheelagh Delaney in Parnell Square, Alun Owen and Harold Pinter in the Eblana and many other lesser writers scattered throughout the city. The great days of the Pike Theatre were coming to an end but there was sufficient energy there to excite my young imagination with Beckett, Genet, Ionesco and other great writers whose influence still resonates fifty years later. They were heady days for this tyro actor, satisfying my need to be connected to this magic world of theatre.

In the midst of all this, however, there was a lack of work that reflected the concerns and fears of a younger generation and its emotional responses to the changes that were even then transforming Irish society and culture. The work I saw always felt removed from the reality that surrounded me in my daily life. James McKenna's *The Scatterin'* was an impressive use of the common vernacular to tell an epic story. Hugh Leonard, by then writing for radio and television, was a voice that was bursting to be heard. His adaptation of James Joyce's *A Portrait of the Artist as a Young Man* into *Stephen D.* was masterly and a highlight of its time. Tom Murphy, rejected by the Abbey, then dominated by Ernest Blythe's philistinism, had become another in the list of exiled writers who must have felt that their work would never be appreciated in their own country. Seán O'Casey sat implacable in Devon, refusing to allow his plays to be performed in the Abbey, 'the cradle of genius' that had created his reputation. It was a bleak time for Irish writers.

Then Brian Friel and his early masterpiece *Philadelphia Here I Come!* burst on the scene and, in one stroke, he changed the nature of the Irish rural play and, in my case, confirmed growing feelings about where my life would lead. While the circumstances of my own life bore only superficial parallels to the world of Gar O'Donnell, I immediately identified with his sense of loneliness, of shyness in the face of emotional distance, of feeling trapped in a place where the real self could not be understood or appreciated.

Friel's genius was to place all these emotional worlds into two aspects of the one person. The play followed the pattern of so many Abbey comedies of the fifties and sixties. There was a kitchen scene, a housekeeper, a parish priest, a frustrated teacher and an uncommunicative father. All the ingredients, in fact, for a pleasant and unmemorable addition to the canon of Irish literature that included writers such as George Shiels, Brinsley McNamara and Lennox Robinson.

Friel, however, subverted the genre with that masterstroke of the same character showing us his public and private selves. The technique allowed us to appreciate the more complex aspects of Gar O'Donnell and the narrow world around him. The heartbreaking relationship between father and son is best demonstrated as S.B. O Donnell, among the most taciturn of men, and Gar Public, equally reticent, shyly sit at the kitchen table on their last night together. Both need to communicate with the other but neither is able to break the pattern of a lifetime. The memories that Gar hoped he shared with his father find no recognition. The sheer agony of the silences, the longing we share with Gar that, for once, his father might say something to remember as he leaves for his new life in Philadelphia seared into my young imagination. Among the other scenes that startled me was the scene where Gar's maternal aunt visits with her husband and dear friend, Ben Burton. The Abbey play *The Country Boy*, by John Murphy, had introduced us to the returning Yank as part of Irish drama but we had never seen anything like Aunt Lizzie, especially as played by the wonderfully named Bee Duffell. Her coarseness, drunkenness and the sense of palpable failure emanating from her exploded the fantasy that everything in the new world would be wonderful and that Gar could escape his many problems by leaving Ireland behind. One of the most devastating lines in the play comes when Aunt Lizzie urges the ever-loyal Ben to encourage Gar to come live with her in America. She expects enthusiasm and excitement. 'What's the difference, Ireland, America, it's just another place to live' is the unexpected reply. How that line struck home to so many of my generation for whom emigration was a distinct possibility.

It wasn't just the theme of the play, its brilliant technique or its compelling characters that changed my young life. No, it was the acting of that first company under Hilton Edwards' magnificent direction that really hit me in the solar plexus. Acting has always been my passion and I can think of no greater gift the gods can bestow on a human than to be an actor. What a subtle power it is to be able to strike an emotional chord with total strangers who sit in darkness drinking in the profound feelings and the deep truths that inform great theatrical art. There have been a number of performances I have seen in my life that stay with me and will haunt me forever. Donal McCann, still sorely missed some years after his untimely death, was responsible for many of them, particularly his masterly *Faith Healer* and *The Steward of Christendom* – his last performance. I will never forget Siobhan McKenna in both *The Cherry Orchard* and *Bailegangaire* or Cyril Cusack as the Shaughran in Boucicault's melodrama of the same name and also in an Abbey production of *The Cherry Orchard*. I could go on and on.

But a special place in my heart is held for that original cast of *Philadelphia*. The incomparable Donal Donnelly and the late Patrick Bedford as the two Gars; that genius of a Kerryman, Eamon Kelly, as the silent S.B.; Mairin D. O'Sullivan as the loyal housekeeper, Madge; and a young and hilarious Eamon Morrissey as the innocent Joe. Together, they formed an ensemble like I had never seen before. In Alpho O'Reilly's divided set, the action of Gar O'Donnell's last night in Ballybeg before his departure for Philadelphia unfolded with a force and an honesty that we had rarely seen in Irish rural drama. Clearly a new voice had arrived in the Irish theatre. Some forty years later, Friel's voice is still clear and vibrant and long may it continue so. That production and the sense that I had found a play that spoke so completely to me simply reinforced my growing belief that, in spite of the many pitfalls of such a life, I had to devote myself to this world where this kind of work was possible.

At the earliest possible opportunity, at eighteen, I applied to the Abbey School of Acting and rejoiced to receive a note of acceptance in February 1967. Recently returned to the Abbey Street location after fifteen years' exile in the Queen's Theatre in Pearse Street, the Abbey was going through some serious issues of transition. With nearly forty years' hindsight, it still seems strange to me that so little of the Abbey repertoire at the Queen's impinged on my youthful theatre-going. Visits to our national theatre were largely confined to the annual Gaelic pantomime, which seemed to me a cut-price version of the ambrosia offered in South King Street. Other than the fun of hearing pop songs translated into Irish and the novelty of seeing a male principal boy in pantomime, few memories of those Abbey visits resonate through the miasma of time.

I still remember with warmth my first exposure to Seán O'Casey with a 1964 production of *The Plough and the Stars.* The ban had been lifted and many of my generation were getting our first glimpse of the work of genius that had both saved the Abbey and inflamed riots in the theatre. Although many years later members of the cast decried that production as not worthy of the Abbey, I remember it as a thing of beauty and power. I still recall the excitement of that amazing language which combined a real sense of Dublin conversation with a heightened, poetic strength. Although my generation was raised to revere the sacrifice of the men of 1916, O'Casey's anger at the futility and the hopelessness of the Republican gesture struck a chord of recognition.

When I joined the Abbey in 1967, it was a strange and frustrating place for many reasons. The management structure was a holdover from the days of iron rule imposed by the still-active Ernest Blythe. Essentially, the board of the Abbey was an executive committee where all decisions concerning programming, casting and other daily details had to be approved by that group. The effect of this was to create a real vacuum at management level, where all decisions had to be referred upwards.

The obsession with the revival of the Irish language as part of the theatre's mission ensured that talented actors who would otherwise have been a valuable part of the company were denied the opportunities they deserved. The punishing schedule of fortnightly rep in the Queen's had left the permanent company exhausted and bitter. It is worth noting that the long sojourn in the Queen's combined with a philistine approach to the art form by management virtually destroyed a whole generation of really talented Irish actors. If Máire Ní Dhomnaill, Angela Newman, Geoffrey and Edward Golden, Pat Layde, Bill Foley and many others did not reach the potential that their abilities deserved, it was the result of a culture in the Abbey that denied them even their own names (all names were translated into Irish for the programme) and never encouraged them to stretch or to explore new techniques. A constant diet of mediocre plays, with occasional productions of Eugene O Neill to leaven the tedium, eroded their spirits and the lack of a realistic career alternative kept many of them in the Abbey long after they should have left to ensure their own artistic growth. That frustration and cynicism spilt over into the work and, for young idealistic actors who felt that change was necessary, the whole situation felt hopeless and shocking.

The new building was significantly different from the Queen's and demanded a very different style of presentation and of acting. Much has been written and spoken about the 'Abbey style of acting', as though it was a specific, carefully documented technique passed from one generation to the next with the solemnity of Holy Scripture. In my many years in the Abbey, I never understood the dynamics of this 'style'. It had a mysterious quality that apparently blessed the elect while the rest of us simply got on with what we knew. The nearest definition came, some years later, from Ulick O'Connor who described it as a 'poetic realism'. Well, that may have been true of the Fay Brothers and their engagement with the works of Yeats and Synge, but no such style has ever been part of any discussion with Abbey actors and directors I have encountered in thirty-five years' connection with that theatre. It is a myth that there was a specific style of acting encouraged in the Abbey and by the mid-sixties the work was sloppy and verging on the amateur.

The first person to really grapple with the scope and the scale of the new theatre was Tomás MacAnna.

Although MacAnna had been part of the theatre since 1948 and was widely seen within the company as Blythe's man, he had a very clear understanding of the need for change and for a repertoire that would embrace the new space and widen the opportunities for the company. MacAnna had spent some time in Europe in the mid-sixties and had developed an interest in the works of Bertolt Brecht, whose theories of alienation had become an integral part of European staging. He had also spent time in America where the first shoots of a new vibrancy in writing and staging were emerging.

Combined with his personal sense of optimism, self-confidence and rebelliousness, MacAnna was the ideal person to oversee the transition from the moribund days of the Queen's to the new theatre with its difficult stage and its fortress-like appearance. When he was appointed artistic advisor in 1966 – it was not until the early seventies that Hugh Hunt became the first artistic director – MacAnna had to use his well-developed sense of guile and subterfuge to get things past a board mired in tradition and longing for an era that was long past its sell by date. He commissioned adaptations of novels that would suit the sprawling nature of the stage, the most successful of which was Brendan Behan's *Borstal Boy*. This was precisely the kind of hit show the Abbey needed. It brought Niall Tóibín back to the Abbey in his signature performance as the older Behan, introduced Frank Grimes, one of the most compelling young Irish actors of the time, as young Brendan and gave countless opportunities to young actors to cut their teeth on the Abbey stage. The international success of that production renewed interest in the Abbey abroad. Looking eastwards, MacAnna invited Madame Knebel from the Moscow Art Theatre to direct *The Cherry Orchard*. He reintroduced Boucicault into the Irish tradition with a magnificent version of *The Shaughran*, directed by Hugh Hunt. He instituted a Gaeltacht tour that brought the Abbey to parts of the country that had never seen professional theatre before. He encouraged a whole new generation of Abbey actors including Donal McCann, Desmond Cave, Robert Carlile, Nuala Hayes, Niall Buggy, Fedelma Cullen, Máire Ní Ghráinne, John Kavanagh and many others, including myself. His departure for the States to lecture at Carleton College, Minnesota, in 1969 brought a mini-golden-period to an end. Neither of his subsequent periods as artistic director matched the excitement and energy of those years in the late sixties when he transformed the fortunes of the national theatre. In this, its centenary year, he deserves to be honoured and fêted for his lifelong devotion to the Old Lady of Abbey Street.

My first foray into direction and administration came in 1970, when, with the encouragement of Hugh Hunt, by then artistic director, I began a theatre-in-education group, together with company colleagues Kathleen Barrington and Nuala Hayes. The Young Abbey was inspired by a movement in Britain where an increasing number of theatres were creating an outreach department specifically to engage school children in the possibilities of drama and the theatre. The combination of performance and improvised work done in a school hall or gymnasium allowed the actors and the students to interact in a dynamic way. It also allowed teachers to use drama as an inter-disciplinary skill, encouraging exploration of history, literature, social sciences and languages through improvisation.

Our early efforts included extracts from well-known Abbey plays linked by a theme that would allow for improvised scenes to be created by the students. 'Up with the Barricades' was an exploration of the impact of the

1916 Rising on Irish life and we included discussion, improvisation and a couple of scenes from O'Casey's work. Later we refined the techniques but the spirit remained the same. We were urging the students to think of issues relating to their own lives through the use of drama and theatre. Although the Young Abbey did not survive the chill winds of fiscal rectitude that characterised the mid-seventies in the Abbey, it was the foundation for Team Theatre Company, which *has* survived to become one of the most influential theatre companies for young people in Europe. This transformation happened because Nuala Hayes, one of the Young Abbey founders and a passionate believer in the power of theatre to change young people's lives, took time out from her acting career to establish the new company and, using skills and techniques she had developed while living in Denmark, she created a whole new approach to theatre-in-education and drama for young people that moved away from the escapism of fairy tales and introduced social and emotional issues for young audiences.

For me, the journey as an actor and director continued until the needs of administration demanded a choice. I opted to focus on being a director, becoming the youngest-ever artistic director of the Abbey, and spent seven years toiling in that particular vineyard until things went very sour. I joined the Gaiety as its artistic and managing director and, with the encouragement of Liam Conroy and Fred O'Donovan, established the Gaiety School of Acting in 1986, an initiative that has had a profound effect on the training of young actors in Ireland and which continues today under the leadership of Patrick Sutton.

In the early nineties, an American career beckoned and the journey took many twists and turns that brought me here to the Upper Mid-West of the United States to head up the Guthrie Theater, the theatre founded by Sir Tyrone Guthrie in 1963. While the journey is not complete, I have come to enjoy the work in this beautiful city in a theatre where it is possible to make real connections with an audience as hungry as I have always been for the power of great theatre. The Guthrie Theater is one of America's most prestigious resident theatres and is now about to embark on an exciting new phase in its distinguished life. In 2006, we will open the New Guthrie Theatre – a three-theatre complex by the banks of the Mississippi that will make this city a centre of theatrical life in the United States. Since coming here in 1996, I have had the opportunity to include many Irish plays in the repertoire. We have done *The Playboy of the Western World*, *The Plough and the Stars*, Hugh Leonard's *Da* and, of course, *Philadelphia, Here I Come!* The circular nature of my journey with that play was profoundly moving when I realised that Brian Friel had written it after spending some time in Minneapolis observing the great Tyrone Guthrie directing his first season here in 1963. As he describes it himself, Friel returned home 'on a Guthrie high' and wrote the play that inspired me to begin my journey in professional theatre. One of the circles in my life was complete.

FIONNUALA FLANAGAN IN THE RTÉ PRODUCTION
OF *AN TRIAIL* BY MÁIRÉAD NÍ GHRÁDA, ADAPTED
FOR TELEVISION FROM THE ORIGINAL STAGE PLAY
IN 1965 AND DIRECTED BY MICHAEL GARVEY.

RTÉ Stills Library.

ALAN TITLEY

NEITHER THE BOGHOLE NOR BERLIN: DRAMA IN THE IRISH LANGUAGE FROM THEN UNTIL NOW

Tennessee Williams once said that good theatre was simply 'great talk'. That being so, one might imagine a great and flourishing theatre in the Irish language, because we are nothing if we are not great talkers. Some of the most artistic and wonderful books in Irish in the twentieth century are hewn out of talk and gab and chat and the incessant flow of never-ending speech. Máirtín Ó Cadhain's great masterpiece *Cré na Cille* is conversation from beginning to end and Tomás Ó Criomhthain's most singular book *Allagar na hInise* is extended gossip. In fact, when the Irish language was being bruised and wrung out during the nineteenth century, it has been said that the act of speaking itself was its only true art form. It may seem strange then that drama in Irish is the poor relation of prose and of poetry, indeed of music and of song, and even now of journalism and of discursive writing.

And a play, like E.M. Forster's novel, must, oh dear, tell a story. And we have been excellent in churning out the stories also, from the early sagas, which unlike the great epics of other literatures were invariably in prose, to the long tale which took several nights to complete, to the pithy short story and anecdote carved with precise verbal care and artistry. We can tell stories and we can talk: why then have we been comparatively limp when it came to writing and producing plays for the theatre and for other media?

We can always plead tradition. Theatre is not an indigenous 'Gaelic' form, although Charles Macklin, a native Irish speaker from Donegal, turned out a fair living in London with his plays in the eighteenth century; ditto and likewise Charles Kelly from Killarney who did in English what he didn't feel able to do in his mother tongue. We can clutch at old thatch straws blowing in the historical wind, such as short plays written and produced in West Kerry in the early nineteenth century, one of which may be as much as four hundred years old. So when Drake was winning seas for England it is just possible that we were prancing on the stage in part of our subdivided kingdoms. And there were always the Ossianic dialogues, the *Laoithe Fiannaíochta*, where Patrick and Oisín argued the toss over the merits of Christianity and paganism in tight quatrains and which were enacted as drama in cottages and cabins all over Ireland for centuries. And the outgrowths of that tradition culminated in long debating poems such as *An Sotach agus a Mháthair* and, more importantly, the magnificent *Cúirt an Mheán Oíche* by Brian Merriman.

In fact the *Cúirt* is a classic example of what might

have been. In a 1984 production in the Peacock Theatre, under the direction of the great Siobhán McKenna, the entire poem was put on the stage without changing one jot of a syllable. Some music was indeed added, but for the rest the poem spoke for itself. The words rang out on the stage and carried the play without any requirement of gimmickry or jiggery-pokery. The rich poetic tradition was merged with verbal magic and with twentieth century production values to create a night of magic and of wonder. We caught a glimpse of what Irish theatre might be. If there had been such a theatre in Limerick in Merriman's time, it is how we imagine he would have wanted it to be; but Limerick then, rather like Limerick now, was hardly a centre of culture.

But lack of a tradition is only a lame excuse. Traditions must begin somewhere. There was a time when Irish poets did not write in syllabic metres. Somebody started it. There was a time when *sean-nós* was new. And beginning a tradition should be an uplifting and a liberating thing, whether starting from nowhere and going somewhere or bursting and ripping apart the tired old things of yesterday. It was done in Spain; it was done in Russia; it was done in England.

What we now have come to call the 'revival period', starting some time in the 1880s, was indeed a time of new dawns. While the prose writers of the revival debated the kind of style and subject matter that was desirable in a new Irish literature, and poetic discourse haggled between the new and the old forms, there was ready agreement that drama had no lineage at all. There was an acceptance, even amongst the more traditional and nativist wings of the literary wars, that drama had to be grafted on with a limb from outside. Although some extremists such as Fr Richard Henebry argued that drama should not be cultivated as it was not a native form, others suggested that it should be modelled on the Ossianic dialogues or on the art of the *seanchaí*. Pearse, for example, urged Irish actors to learn their art from the storytellers of the Gaeltacht, although we can forgive him anything because of his admission that it never occurred to him to read Kickham. Nonetheless, it was generally accepted that, as one writer put it: 'in this matter of creation of an Irish stage extreme insularity will retard instead of serve the cause'.

It wasn't as if so-called native forms were left untended. One of the most popular forms of Irish theatre, particularly in Gaeltacht areas and at the annual literary festival of An tOireachtas, is the *agallamh beirte* or humorous dialogue. This is a form of theatre where two actors perform a verbal duel on some current topic in a simple verse form. Although initially much of this was done extempore, it is now usually well rehearsed, though nonetheless witty and entertaining for all that. This mixture of poetry, repartee and theatricality is still attractive but remains at the foothills of dramatic action. Amateur theatre has also been to the fore in presenting adaptations of older Irish legends and might well be responsible for a form of art which is uncommon elsewhere. We might call this the *scéaldráma* or the 'dramatised story', where the actors re-enact a Fenian tale in a mixture of 'telling' and 'showing'. Chuck in some dancing and song and horseplay, and you get very close to a drama, properly so called.

That drama 'properly-so-called' had a rough beginning. When Seán Ó Tuama wrote his *Gunna Cam agus Slabhra Óir* in 1964, he said that he had no real model to draw on, only Shakespeare. Thus, it is a historical drama, in three acts, in a mixture of verse and prose, set in a castle, with quasi-historical characters complete with monologues, asides and soliloquys, but without any ghost. It is beautifully written and carefully modulated, and rises and falls in dramatic tension, as any good play should do. It also had the attraction of being a palimpsest of our civil war, a subject still touchy enough at the time to be only approached with caution. But its artistry and stagecraft showed how far drama in Irish had come since another historical production of *Eoghan Ruadh Ua Néill* produced in Maynooth in 1906. It was a five-act play with a cast of twenty, which ran for more than five hours. And despite the clerical students' desire for any kind of entertainment which smacked of the outside world, it must surely have put them off theatre for life.

Not as bad, however, as a play that was penned three years earlier which had forty-three characters, eighteen different scenes and would have lasted for eight hours if it had been ever produced, or An tAthair Peadar Ó Laoire's *Niamh*, which had speeches that went on for five pages of densely packed print.

For all their desire to imitate French or Russian models in theory, the early Irish dramatists mostly aped the English melodrama in its Anglo-Irish corrupted form. As with many plays in the Abbey style, for many plays in Irish the kitchen and the yard beyond became the centre of the universe and the extent of the known world. Plays with titles such as *Prátaí Mhicil Thaidhg* ('Mike Ted's Potatoes') or *Caismirt na gCearc* ('The Battle of the Hens') or *Cupán Tae Airt* ('Art's Cup of Tea') were not likely to convince audiences that they were in the vanguard of a modern movement, while my own favourite, *Bó i bPoll* ('A Cow in a Hole'), required the beast to be on the stage with a wave flowing over it and seven men hauling her out with ropes and sacks, and all of this in the days of severe realism without the benefit of video or flashy technical effects.

For all that, these plays were a novelty. It was the first time that Irish-speakers had seen themselves on the stage speaking in their own language, and it was the first time many of them had ever seen a play at all. It is also true that many of the leaders of the Anglo-Irish dramatic revival were sympathetic to, and supportive of, theatre in the Irish language. Lady Gregory, Edward Martyn and the Fay brothers were all enthusiasts and provided practical, artistic and financial support in differing degrees. Even Yeats himself descended from on high and encouraged playwrights of the Gaelic League to focus 'on the treasures of the Irish language', and just because Yeats said it did not mean that it was necessarily to be rejected. There is no doubt that the same baneful influence of the peasant play dominated the Irish-language theatre for some time. When models were looked for they were found in the rompings of the new stage. While Edward Martyn urged the need for translations from the great well of European literature to be an inspiration to Irish playwrights, they preferred for many years to splash around in the puddle of translations of Synge and T.C. Murray and Lennox Robinson.

And yet, slowly, a new dramatic tradition was being forged. It is interesting that virtually no important writer in Irish is primarily known for his or her work as a dramatist. Pádraic Ó Conaire's work for the theatre was pretty disastrous. Máirtín Ó Cadhain, for all his brilliance with conversation, a brilliance which has been matchless and untouchable in any of our two languages, crashed dramatically when he attempted theatre. Seosamh Mac Grianna translated, as did his brother Séamas, but they never tried an original. Eoghan Ó Tuairisc wrote important works for the theatre, but he remains primarily a novelist and a poet. Críostóir Ó Floinn has come closest, but he may have been too eclectic for his own career. Máiréad Ní Ghráda was one of the few who stuck to her craft as a playwright and eschewed the temptations of the other forms. In fact, there are very few of the important writers of the twentieth century who didn't have a go at writing for the stage – Caitlín Maude, Michael Hartnett, Liam Ó Muirthile, Éilís Ní Dhuibhne – but we can hardly say of them that it was their primary concern.

It may be that there is something mysterious and special about writing for the stage or, indeed, about writing a radio or television play. The world is replete with examples of great writers of one genre that do not transfer to another. Hugh Leonard, a great playwright but an indifferent novelist; Tom Murphy likewise; John McGahern vice versa; and Edna O'Brien similarly around. But writing in Irish has always presented another difficulty, and it is a difficulty that has nothing to do with the airy-fairy world of tradition or of what is right and proper and appropriate and suitable for an Irish play to be, and is away beyond the critical-cum-metaphysical debates that we like to engage in as play-goers or writers or interested viewers.

The Irish-language playwright, and actor, and director, is plagued with practical uncertainty. He, or she, is also squeezed between the uncertainty of a definite audience and the requirement to develop one.

There have been high points in this development of a literate and appreciative audience, and there have been long and stretching deserts of neglect. Almost at random, a glance through the programme of the Abbey Theatre shows us that for the season of November 1924 to May

1925, in a period of seven months, nineteen plays in Irish were produced on the Abbey stage. Although many of these were one-acters, and a goodly number were translations, it must be presumed that there were sufficient of a high standard to continue a similar policy over the next decade. In the season of 1937–38, we find twenty-two Irish-language plays being produced in the Peacock, and in the same year two other plays, including Douglas Hyde's seminal *Casadh an tSúgáin* – initially premiered in the Gaiety along with Yeats and George Moore's *Diarmuid and Grania* by the Irish Literary Theatre in 1901 – were performed on the main stage. This was no small beer or even cheap plonk. Excepting the Abbey classics necessarily revived for Ireland and for tourists, this was good theatre.

But for every fall there is a wake. Although the Abbey's retreat from Irish-language theatre was not, so to speak, dramatic, it was certain and slow and sure-footed. Its place was taken by the Damer Theatre in Dublin, run by An Club Drámaíochta and sponsored by Gael-Linn. Between 1955 and 1970 they produced the best and most revolutionary of Irish theatre. There were, of course, translations, from Dutch, French, English, Welsh, Spanish, Russian – theatre that was a long wail from 'the cow in the well and the fairy in the fort', as one commentator characterised the revival period. More importantly, there were the most serious plays of Seán Ó Tuama (usually premiered in Cork), Eoghan Ó Tuairisc, Críostóir Ó Floinn and Máiréad Ní Ghráda, which provided the most sustained period of original and creative theatre ever in Irish between the mid-sixties and the early seventies. The Damer also performed the first production of Brendan Behan's *An Giall* in 1958, before it became padded and paddy-fied in London by Joan

Littlewood some years later. It is also worth mentioning that an international actor such as Niall Tóibín, whose father Seán translated many plays into Irish, cut his dramatic teeth in the Damer which helped to launch his career.

Máiréad Ní Ghráda's *An Triail* also received its first production in the Damer and, in spite of the wonderful tribute paid by Harold Hobson, the drama critic of the English *Sunday Times* when he reviewed it as part of the Dublin Theatre Festival, it remains the most harrowing yet sympathetic examination of the unmarried mother in Ireland and her savage treatment by society and by the Magdalen laundries. Máiréad Ní Ghráda could not have known the real and abiding horror of those places of iniquitous punishment and horrific self-righteousness, and yet her imagination invented a fraction of the awfulness of those times, lifting the spotted and stained veil on an Ireland which we willingly and wittingly hid from view.

Both the early Abbey and the later Peacock, and beyond that the ever-inventive Damer, provided work for Irish-language actors and directors and writers. There was a certain confidence that if, as a writer — and writers are the most central and important creatures of the entire dramatic enterprise — you had wares to sell there was a market in which you could sell them. Be a half-decent writer and there is a half-chance that your work will at least be half-considered for production, and those odds are not half-bad. But after the Damer folded up its underground tent, largely for administrative and managerial reasons, a much bigger famine returned than ever before.

There was always, of course, life outside Dublin, particularly with the amateur movement in the Gaeltacht.

The most consistently successful of those theatres was Amharclann Ghaoth Dobhair in the heart of the Donegal Gaeltacht, which both cultivated local writers and actors and welcomed visiting troupes of players. Professionally Galway's Taibhdhearc Theatre was almost as lively and as innovative as the Abbey was at its best and its first few seasons saw productions by that self-invented Corkman without a drop of Irish blood in his thespian veins, Micheál MacLíammóir. He wrote, translated, directed and sought out plays of a high order and intensity for this theatre in the 1920s and '30s and showed how one deeply passionate and driven man could light a flame where only darkness reigned before. The Taibhdhearc did have the advantage of being on the edge of, and in those years more or less surrounded by, the largest Gaeltacht in the country and could marry the urban with the rural as well as the national with the international. It has been a long time now since plays by Sierra Martinez or Eca de Queiroz or Gheón or Jalabert or Karel Capek were produced on any stage in Ireland; yet these were the staple diet of the rich programme offered by An Taibhdhearc for many years.

So the story of theatre in Irish during this last hundred years has been a patchy and bitty one. From uncertain beginnings it flourished with great energy for the first decades of the new state, went into some decline, burned brightly again during the heydays of the Damer and almost vanished for periods during the 1970s and '80s. One bright light during those years was, undoubtedly, the regular Saturday-night radio play, 'Dráma an tSathairn', produced by Seán Ó Briain. It was the only regular outlet for writers, and indeed for actors, who wished to continue working in Irish. Although a radio play can be a very different thing from the fully fledged stage production, it does have its connections with our main concern. Louis McNeice said that 'sound radio can do things that no other medium can and if "sound" dies, those things will not be done'. He was referring to the primacy of the word, which is, in a sense, where we came in, with the Irish love of talk and of the emphasis on speech and language often for its own sake. But these radio dramas had a further importance.

They were probably listened to by some thousands of people every Saturday night. It would take many weeks of packing the Peacock or the Taibhdhearc, not to mention the Mint or any of the smaller studio theatres in which many Irish plays are produced, before you would get anything like the audience you would have for a radio play. They also trained a whole generation of people to listen; and by listening to fill the magical and enigmatic margin between themselves and the play with their imagination. Works which were originally written for the stage but had no chance of production because of the dire lack of a decent theatre often began their life on the radio, and works originally written for the radio made successful transmigrations to the stage.

One of those plays might be, for example, Siobhán Ní Shúilleabháin's very accomplished *Cití*, first produced on the radio in 1975. It tells the story of a young girl in the Kerry Gaeltacht who falls in love with an Englishman during the making of a film in the area, which we must presume to be *Ryan's Daughter*. It is a beautifully crafted story about culture clash and the incommensurabilities of romanticisms. She wants to escape from her boghole beyond Dingle to the flashy city of London, and he wishes to swap the urban rat race for a quiet little home in the west. But Siobhán Ní Shúilleabháin employs a whole battery of devices, from internal monologues through flashbacks and snappy dialogue, but, most tellingly, using a stream of commentary from the bitchy old gossips of the community to emphasise the horror from which Cití is trying to escape and which her husband can never be part of. The narrow stranglehold of the rural community was ever a theme for playwrights, but one suspects if this play had been written by some other hand twenty years previously it would have got the straight-up treatment with the cow in the yard and the fairy in the fort and grim realism reaping its havoc. Exposure to international theatre and to other media prepared play-writing in Irish for a great leap forward, if such was to happen.

There were always, of course, writers who were willing to play with the form and to do this in a bold and courageous fashion. One of these was Críostóir Ó Floinn, who penned a string of successful plays in the 1960s and '70s culminating, in my mind, with *Mise Raifteirí an File* in 1973. Historical plays were always popular, if not always successful, but Ó Floinn manages to mix the story of blind Raftery with the cultural debates that took place at the turn of the twentieth century and with our later literary wars. Apart from Raftery the cast includes Lady Gregory, Dr Mahaffy (former Provost of Trinity College), Douglas Hyde, Frank O'Connor, Sceach Áth Cinn, or the Headford Bush, and even Death himself. This gives an idea of the range and scope of the work, but Ó Floinn, being the master he was, never lets the culture clog up the story or history slow down the action. He never subordinates a 'message' to the essential work of providing dramatic sustenance, and even if he did, then the theatre can survive and thrive on that too.

My own *Tagann Godot* or 'Godot Turns Up' was a sequel to Beckett's great play, and I was privileged in it being produced by Tomás Mac Anna in the Abbey/Peacock in 1990. I was also privileged in it having the blessing, well, at least the tolerance, of Beckett himself. Mac Anna was one of the geniuses of the Irish stage and shaped the Irish-language policy of the Abbey Theatre for at least half a century and mostly against the tide.

One of the most successful and most serious and sustained attempts to develop a proper professional theatre in recent years was the venture of Amharclann de hÍde. Founded in 1992, it was young, ambitious and creative. There is nothing it did not try. Clíona Ní Anluain drove it from the beginning, and her energy and creativity was later augmented and validated by Bríd Ní Ghallchóir.

Experimental plays such as Liam Ó Muirthile's *Tine Chnámh* utilised dance and music and poetry. The straight conventional play and the wildly unusual followed one another. They urged writers who had never written plays before or had not written plays in Irish, such as Michael Harding and Éilís Ní Dhuibhne, to come up with the goods, which they did. They did public readings and organised workshops. They adapted stories and novels when necessary. They used new actors; they trained them; they did pure Gaeltacht theatre in uncompromising language and dialect; they worked bilingually when the occasion demanded; their productions were lavish when required and bared to the essentials when necessary. In fact, if one were to draw up a list of requirements for an Irish-language theatre and put all the complaints into the pot, it would have to be said that they met them all, over a ten-year period. And yet, they too went out of business.

Prescinding entirely from the normal urge of artistic directors to move on and to do something else, they were dogged by the old problem of lack of certain continuity and a definite home. Originally financed by Bord na

Gaeilge for a time, they became squeezed in the politics of money between the Bord and the Arts Council. For all their innovations, they were living from year to year and from hand to mouth. They needed the luxury of the comfort of failure, such as the Abbey Theatre has. They discovered that thinking big was no substitute for funding agencies acting small. Theatre is supposed to land a punch, but that is difficult to do if you are lying on the floor.

There is a Japanese story about a man travelling the country seeking out the greatest archer in the land. He comes to a village and spots some targets with arrows stuck straight into the bull's-eyes. When he asks who shot those arrows he is told it was a madman. When he inquires further about how this came about he is given the very simple explanation: 'Well, first he fired the arrows, and then he drew the targets.'

Drama acts first and then seeks out its audience. It is a form of articulation proudly below poetry and beyond the reach of newspaper stuff. It shows us at our most stupid and crass and evil and vain and ridiculous; and maybe, just maybe, drama in Irish was not quite ready to make this mad leap. And even if it did, drama is also an art of compromise. You can write poetry or a novel and, apart from finicky editors, you can get away with more or less what you like. Poetry, after all, is the excresence of the soul, and not many are going to get involved in that ectoplasmic mess. Prose can float away on the everyday and has a latitude and a girth which is difficult to reduce. Drama, on the other hand, enacts the whole mess of what we are. It sometimes has to be raw and ugly in order to be smooth and beautiful. It can indulge itself in great emotional orgies and provide religious experience without the prayers.

It is the extreme subjectivity of art that makes it art;

it is the idiosyncracy which makes it good; it is the intensity of imagination that makes it different from life. But drama in Irish has never had the opportunity to take these chances. There is no theatre that the author can attach himself to and be reasonably sure that his company will have a go for him next time around. And the theatre will wish to please several writers. And the director will change and the policy will alter. And the actors will be scratching themselves waiting for work. And everybody will be cautious and quiet and careful. At its best, drama should be cooking with burning oil; unfortunately, we more often get a rightly timed microwave ready-meal, safely wrapped in tinfoil.

And the audience will sit at home watching TV. And, undoubtedly, they will see one of the best home-grown Irish soaps in any language on TG4, *Ros na Rún* – as they heard the quirky, funny, off-the-rocks and yet socially relevant *Baile an Droichid* by Joe Steve Ó Neachtain on Raidió na Gaeltachta. There are more opportunities now for writers and producers on television and on radio than for many years. Cathal Póirtéir has successfully revived radio drama in RTÉ, and TG4 have plans for short films and for plays. And although these link to live theatre, they are not the same thing.

That great Scottish actor Brian Cox once asked a fellow actor why they did what they did and why did people come and watch them in the theatre. The reply he got was: 'It's energy, we provide energy for others, people who are tired and sit and watch and get a boost from our energy.'

And theatre in Irish provides energy for Irish, just as it provides energy for the imagination. The theatre and the language require both.

CONOR MOLONEY AND DAVID WILMOT IN THE
ROYAL SHAKESPEARE COMPANY PRODUCTION
OF *THE LIEUTENANT OF INISHMORE* BY MARTIN
MCDONAGH, DIRECTED BY WILSON MILAM
AND DESIGNED BY FRANCIS O'CONNOR.

Royal Shakespeare Company. Photo: Hugo Glendinning.

Anthony Roche

The 'Irish' Play on the London Stage 1990–2004

What might be termed the internationalisation of Irish drama was begun in 1990 by the phenomenal success of Brian Friel's *Dancing at Lughnasa*. With this play, Friel broke his association with Field Day, the Derry-based theatre company he had co-founded ten years earlier with Stephen Rea, and sought the greater resources of producer Noel Pearson and Dublin's Abbey Theatre, where the play was first staged in May 1990 in a production by Patrick Mason and with the memorable 'field of wheat' design by Joe Vanek. It opened to mixed notices and reasonable houses at the Abbey, but then began to build and build as audiences took to heart and responded powerfully to Friel's moving dramatisation of the plight of these five 'brave' Donegal women of the 1930s. *Lughnasa* went on to even greater acclaim in London and New

York, where it was awarded a Tony for Best Play in 1991. Its success helped to create a fashionable trend for Irish plays in both capitals in the period since. That success in New York was fitful, as the subsequent short-lived run of Friel's *Wonderful Tennessee* proved. But ever since *Lughnasa* the Irish play on the London stage has become a major factor in the cultural lives of both countries, what has been termed 'a distinct and distinctly marketable phenomenon'. It is on that phenomenon I would like to concentrate for the course of this talk.

Where a century earlier Irish playwrights such as Wilde and Shaw had provided sparkling comedies for the London stage, their plays drew their characters and settings exclusively from English society. The difference registered by Wilde and Shaw's Irishness was conveyed by a more objective, detached, ironic attitude to the treatment of their material. But the founding of the Abbey a hundred years ago led to a self-consciously Irish subject matter, one it has proved difficult to move beyond, especially in relation to non-Irish audiences. Above all, there was the decision to set Irish plays in a rural rather than an urban or a suburban setting, and the cottage locale has remained a mainstay ever since. One of the most potent sources of *Lughnasa's* appeal to non-Irish audiences is the stage image of an Irish cottage kitchen in the 1930s with not one but five colleens baking, sewing and generally generating *craic*, against the visual backdrop of a huge golden wheatfield and the verbal aura of the narrator's childish wonderment. The play is set in the historic past and offers consoling, nostalgic, unified images of Irishness, however troubling its verbal content may be. Its very success raises the problems associated with writing an 'Irish' play, with what delineates an on-stage definition of 'Irishness'.

Thomas Kilroy has written of the incident which gave rise to *Dancing at Lughnasa*. He and Friel were attending the première of the latter's dramatisation of Turgenev's *Fathers and Sons* at London's Royal National Theatre in 1988. During a break, they and their wives crossed the bridge over the River Thames beside the National Theatre and heard the voices of the homeless as they were settling down for the night on the Embankment. Among these, Irish voices were discernible. Friel suddenly began to speak of how two of his aunts had ended up like that, of how as a young man he came to London to search for the two family members who had gone missing from Donegal many years before. As Kilroy puts it: 'What he found was destitution.' This autobiographical incident surfaces in the play in Michael's monologue of how his aunts Agnes and Rose left Ballybeg mere days after the events recorded in the play and how years later he went to find them: 'They took to drink; slept in parks, in doorways, on the Thames Embankment. Then Agnes died of exposure. And two days after I found Rose in that grim hospice – she didn't recognize me, of course – she died in her sleep.' England is also the place from which Gerry Evans comes and to which he returns, the place, as it turns out, where he is maintaining a second family. But England, its destitution and its otherness are only verbally conjured in *Dancing at Lughnasa*; the play itself is set just before the fall.

If Friel has kept the dramatic emphasis in *Lughnasa* on a rural Irish setting while England remains off-stage, Frank McGuinness has used the staging of his plays in London to represent the cultural, political and historical exchanges between the Irish and the English. *Someone Who'll Watch Over Me* premièred at the Hampstead Theatre Club in the summer of 1992 and went on to subsequent successful productions at the Abbey in Dublin and on

Broadway. Its tale of three Western hostages held prisoner in Beirut resonated off the real-life incarceration of Brian Keenan and John McCarthy. In so emphatically identifying its sole three characters as an Irishman, an Englishman and an American, McGuinness was clearly writing a play of contending national identities and doing a great deal in the process to confront and challenge racial stereotypes. The Irishman in particular is extremely hostile when the Englishman is introduced into the space he and the American have established. But his macho patronising crumbles when the American is taken away and he finds a comfort in the gentleness of the Englishman he has earlier derided. The mutual stripping away of defences was not done in any po-faced way but with a sense of outrageous fun and fantasy. And the play's confrontation of the enemy within had much to say about the nature and development of Anglo-Irish relations during the 1990s. McGuinness's *Mutabilitie*, staged at the Royal National Theatre in 1997, was an ambitious attempt to stage the meeting between cultures during the Elizabethan plantation of Ireland. It centred on the poet Edmund Spenser's troubled time as a coloniser in Cork and a brief (and hitherto unrecorded) visit by William Shakespeare and two fellow actors to these shores. In the London production by Trevor Nunn, the effect was rather of Celtic pantomime. In a later Dublin production, by Michael Caven, the stage was largely stripped, with only the necessary props and atmospheric lighting. This threw the emphasis on the characters and their predicaments; it also shifted the home ground, as it were, from English to Irish, with the Englishmen consequently much more under threat.

Now, I have mentioned the cases of two Irish playwrights having their work produced on a London stage. I am conscious as I say so that Brian Friel was born in Omagh, resided in Derry and now lives in Donegal, and that Frank McGuinness was born in Buncrana in County Donegal and now lives in Dublin; that they both come from a county uniquely situated in relation to Ireland north and south. But the next playwright I wish to discuss presents an even more complex background. Martin McDonagh is the figure who raises most of all the issues surrounding the recent development of the Irish play in London. He does so in part because his own background throws into question any easy assumptions about national origins. The son of *émigré* Irish parents, McDonagh was born and raised in London. When asked in a 1998 RTÉ documentary why he chose to set his plays in the west of Ireland, he replied that he had tried writing plays set in London and America, but without success. It was when he recalled the setting and conversations from his summer visits as a child to relatives in the west of Ireland that he found his dramatic idiom, 'close to home but distant', as he put it. His initial success was gained by the staging of *The Beauty Queen of Leenane* in 1996. As befits a child of the Irish diaspora, its staging could not be confined to either Ireland or England but was a joint production by Galway's Druid and London's Royal Court, directed by Garry Hynes, premièred to open Galway's new Town Hall in 1996 and subsequently transferring to London's Royal Court. This process was replicated when *The Beauty Queen* was restaged with the other two plays in what has become known as 'The Leenane Trilogy', *A Skull in Connemara* and *The Lonesome West*, in June and July of 1997. McDonagh's plays are characterised by black humour and brutal violence. This has proved a commercially winning combination, leaving packed audiences rocking with laughter and responding with a standing ovation, as I saw on the night his *Cripple of Inishmaan* transferred to a much bigger London stage. But McDonagh's success in London, New York and elsewhere worldwide has also generated unease that the audiences' laughter is provoked by the near-psychotic antics of characters purporting to be Irish, that McDonagh's bizarre and surreal dramas – products of his own overheated imagination – are set in recognisable Irish localities in the west of Ireland such as Leenane and Inishmaan, and that all of this is offered up on London stages as the re-emergence of the 'stage Irish' stereotype which the Irish theatre movement has done so much to overcome and to banish.

The arguments surrounding McDonagh's emergence in the 1990s uncannily replicate those which greeted the première of Synge's *Playboy of the Western World* almost a century earlier. The objection is that both playwrights are outsiders from the west of Ireland community they claim to represent, that they identify a propensity to violence in their characters and that those people are exaggerated into grotesque caricatures. Although McDonagh proclaimed that his primary interest was in movies, the evidence of his plays suggests a deep knowledge of theatre and of classic Irish theatre at that, in particular the plays of Synge. The title of *The Lonesome West* directly quotes from Pegeen's father in *The Playboy*: 'Oh, there's sainted glory this day in the lonesome west.' And when a character in *A Skull in Connemara* has a spade driven into his skull and then returns to say he's not dead yet, we are clearly in the vicinity of Synge's father-and-son parricidal conflict. It is no coincidence that the original director of McDonagh's Leenane trilogy, Garry Hynes, should be the one whose trailblazing production of Synge's masterpiece in the 1980s brought the latter to theatrical life and interest again.

But McDonagh is not content to reference classic Irish drama and so place himself comfortably in that tradition. Part of his plays' unsettling, postmodern effect is that they mix high and low elements in an unsettling way. The mother and daughter in *The Beauty Queen of Leenane* recall Mommo and her two granddaughters in Tom Murphy's *Bailegangaire* in their verbal altercations and their entrapment within an archaic peasant cottage; but the sheer level of physical and psychological torture, especially the scene where Maureen pours boiling oil over Mag, brings us closer to the camp melodrama of a Hollywood movie like *Whatever Happened to Baby Jane?* And if the endlessly squabbling brothers Coleman and Valene in *The Lonesome West* recall many of the male double acts in Irish theatre, whether O'Casey's Joxer and the Captain or Beckett's two tramps, the prissiness of one and the unregenerate slobbishness of the other are straight out of Neil Simon's *The Odd Couple*. There is no clear time frame for McDonagh's plays: they draw on images from traditional Irish plays of decades past, particularly the rural cottage setting. But their younger characters endlessly discuss characters and scenes from popular 1970s American TV series, and other references indicate a more contemporary provenance. The plays work with a calculated cunning and an utter lack of sentimentality, towards the Irish theatrical canon as much as anything else.

His more recently staged play, *The Lieutenant of Inishmore*, was rejected by both Druid and London's National Theatre before being accepted and staged by the Royal Shakespeare Company, first at Stratford in 2001, then in London's West End the following year, which is where I saw it. The experience of seeing this 'Irish' play on the London stage was a disturbing one and I came out onto the London streets in two minds. The play had featured scenes of violence and cruelty beyond anything in the earlier work, one in particular involving the on-stage dismemberment of bloody torsos. The extreme republican Padraic broke off his torture of an alleged drug-pusher (see illustration, p. 127) to take a domestic phone call concerning the illness of his cat, 'Wee Thomas', which ended up with the torture victim having to console his torturer. So this was clearly the most extreme of McDonagh's plays. But it was also the funniest and, even when I closed my eyes during the most violent scenes, I continued to laugh at the verbal exchanges, the overlapping, elliptical, self-reflexive idiom that McDonagh has perfected, where the most awful doings are accompanied by a tone of sweet reasonableness and outraged innocence. It was also clear that McDonagh was directing his satiric aim at extreme republican violence and its increasing normalisation and doing so not through the respectable medium of tragedy or documentary realism but through uproarious and ever-more-outrageous farce. For all of these reasons, I felt sure that *The Lieutenant of Inishmore* would never have an Irish production. It did, however, play there in a touring production by the RSC during the first week of the 2003 Dublin Theatre Festival. Which raises the question of audiences and the overly general assumptions made about them. The London performance of McDonagh's play was notable for the relatively large number of Irish people in the audience; and they did not seem to be reacting in any markedly different way from the others. Indeed, audiences in Dublin responded by turning out in great numbers and reacting with laughter to both the trilogy and *The Lieutenant*; some would see this as evidence of how thoroughly colonised we still remain. What was striking about the Irish audiences McDonagh drew was that many of them were young and few of them could be characterised as 'regular theatre-goers'. But the supply of the latter is ageing and dwindling; and the Abbey for one is concerned to build and broaden its support base, as the centenary production of Boucicault's *The Shaughraun* demonstrates. My own feeling is that the smash-and-grab theatrics of Martin McDonagh have, in their phenomenal impact in Ireland and throughout the world, changed the landscape of the 'Irish' play irrevocably.

The other major dramaturgic development of the past ten years or so that has very much featured on the Dublin and London stages is the rise of the monologue play, in which characters are usually alone on stage addressing the audience in a more direct fashion than usual. In such plays, even when more than one character is present, they usually remain unaware of or do not acknowledge each other. The great original of the form is Brian Friel's *Faith Healer*, the success of whose 1980 Abbey production redressed its failure the year before on Broadway. In the play, the three characters – Frank Hardy the Faith Healer, his wife/mistress Grace and his cockney manager Teddy – all directly address themselves to the audience and give varying accounts of their lives together on the road. Not all the incidents match up. Did Grace give birth to a dead child in Kinlochbervie? If so, Frank never mentions it. And what precisely occurred on the night of their homecoming to Ireland? Whatever the detail, the outcome was the death of Frank Hardy and the subsequent suicide of Grace, all of which establishes that these figures are ghosts, revenants, forced to live on in the limbo of the stage and to tell their stories to the only ones who will listen, the audience. In 1994, Friel returned to the form for his play *Molly Sweeney*, which premièred at the Gate and went on to play in London's Almeida

Theatre. He now makes the woman the centre of the triad. The blind Molly's monologues convey her distinctive perceptions of the world around her, both before and after she is cured. The monologue play can be said to provide a kind of liberation from the more familiar and stereotypical visual constraints of the 'Irish' play, in particular the rural cottage. In *Faith Healer* the only minimal visual emblems of Irishness are Frank Hardy's green socks. It owns up to the fact that we are in a theatre rather than in what passes for reality, and draws the audience into close relation with the on-stage character. The intimacy of the exchange allows the character to furnish an account of themselves which, however self-serving it may be, does not allow external impressions to dominate. In turn, the audience gains direct access to their innermost thoughts and feelings.

The chief exponent of the monologue play is the young Dublin playwright Conor McPherson. A graduate of UCD, he began writing, acting and directing plays while at college and continued afterwards to stage his own work with the company he had co-founded in such venues as the City Arts Centre and the International Bar. Despite his best efforts, McPherson's plays were not picked up on by the Dublin theatre establishment and it was to the London stage that he owed his breakthrough as one of the most important and exciting of the younger Irish playwrights. McPherson has clearly been influenced by Friel's *Faith Healer* and draws on its structure of four interlocking monologues for his breakthrough play, *This Lime Tree Bower*, where separate stories of working-class Northsiders and well-to-do Southsiders eventually come into collision. McPherson has forged a distinctive Dublin idiom, tough yet with a vein of lyricism, for plays of contemporary urban experience represented in monologue form. When London's Royal Court Theatre commissioned a play from McPherson, the hugely successful *The Weir*, they made it a condition that the play not be in monologue form. Did they also suggest to this most urban of contemporary Irish playwrights that he opt for the most traditional and recognisably 'Irish' dramatic ingredients: a rural pub where old men sit, drink and tell stories of supernatural occurrences? But McPherson's distinctive handling of monologue remains central to *The Weir*'s dramatic achievement, as each of the four characters in turn tells a story dealing with life-and-death issues and playing on the fear of the irrational in human behaviour. The last monologue, where the young woman responds to the three old men by telling them of her daughter's recent death by drowning and of a communication from beyond the grave, turns the tables and most disturbingly raises the question: is it true? There is nothing finally to provide ultimate verification, nothing but the words as spoken on the stage. Though none of his plays has quite enjoyed the success of *The Weir*, this has enabled McPherson to reclaim his urban terrain in such works as *Port Authority*, which uses a young, a middle-aged and an old man to explore three utterly different social strata of contemporary Dublin. McPherson's plays now emerge as co-productions between London's Royal Court and Dublin's Gate theatres. In his latest, *Shining City*, the two central male characters at times share the stage; but one is a patient telling his story to a listening therapist, so the monologue form is retained.

The 2004 London season also saw Sebastian Barry's *Whistling Psyche*, a monologue play which brought together two late-Victorian women in an English railway station at night. One was the iconic Florence Nightingale; the other the extraordinarily exotic creation James Miranda Barry, the woman who masqueraded as a man to become a doctor. As in all of the plays on his family history, Sebastian Barry focuses on the Cork origins of his namesake and develops the notion of 'Irishness' as a category which can travel, metamorphose and change identity. At one point, Dr James Miranda Barry describes himself/herself as a hybrid, 'that other sort of creature, neither white nor black, nor brown nor even green, but the strange original that is an Irish person'. As I started this talk with the translation in 1990 of Brian Friel's *Dancing at Lughnasa* with its Irish production and provenance to a London stage, I draw to my conclusion in 2004 with the Almeida production of Sebastian Barry's latest play, where Dr Barry is played by the extraordinary actress Kathryn Hunter, and where the stage and personnel are English not Irish.

The notable omission from my survey has been plays which engage in representational terms with the Irish present. Again, Brian Friel has been to the fore in this respect in the 1990s, responding to the reception of *Lughnasa* with two plays which faced into the uncertainty of the Irish present, *Wonderful Tennessee* and *Give Me Your Answer, Do!* The Ireland they depict is now one of material prosperity, but it is also a post-Catholic Ireland marked by spiritual uncertainty. These plays have had less acclaim both at home and abroad than *Lughnasa*, but they show Friel's refusal to rest content with what he has already achieved. His greatest success on the London stage in recent years has been as a translator and interpreter of Chekhov. Friel's version of *Uncle Vanya* and his dramatisation in *Afterplay* of the subsequent brief encounter in Moscow between two characters from separate Chekhov plays both enjoyed successful productions there in 2002.

Of the younger Irish playwrights dramatising a different contemporary Irish reality, Rough Magic's Declan Hughes has written of the reception in London in the early 1990s of his breakthrough play, *Digging for Fire*: 'In 1992 a friend of mine took the editor of a men's style magazine to a performance of *Digging for Fire* at the Bush Theatre in London. At the interval, this career *Zeitgeist* surfer turned to my friend and said, "I didn't think they *had* people like that in Ireland."' Londoners' surprise at seeing sophisticated urban thirty-somethings in an Irish rather than an English or American setting soon wore off, however, and subsequent plays by Declan Hughes and other younger writers who sought to show contemporary images of Irishness found less of a welcome on the London stage. There have recently been rumblings against the ubiquity of the monologue play in both London and Dublin. And a London reviewer in 2000 responded with some asperity when faced with yet another 'Irish' play: 'It makes me wonder what kind of postcolonial transaction is going on as I sit in the Royal Court's magnificent new upholstery, watching those wild Irish Yahoos, again.' The London stage proved particularly hospitable to Marie Jones' *Stones in His Pockets*, an entertaining play on Irish character with its two male actors playing all the parts; but that play has recently closed, admittedly after an extraordinary run. If the 'Irish' play came into fashion on the London stage around 1990, then it may well be going out of fashion some fourteen years later. That phenomenon has already left its mark and will continue to influence whatever Irish playwrights choose to write in the near future, whether they seek to capture that success again or to write in determined reaction against it.

NOTES ON CONTRIBUTORS

CHRISTOPHER FITZ-SIMON is a former Literary Manager and Artistic Director of the Abbey Theatre, and Artistic Director of the Irish Theatre Company. His chief books are *The Boys* (a biography of Micheál MacLíammóir and Hilton Edwards, 1994) and *The Abbey Theatre* (2003). He has written many plays for BBC and RTÉ, as well as dramatisations from Bowen, Forzano, Giraudoux, Joyce, Stoker, Wilde, and so on.

NICHOLAS GRENE is Professor of English Literature at Trinity College, Dublin. He has lectured widely on Irish literature abroad. He is the author of *Synge: A Critical Study of the Plays* (1975), *Shakespeare, Jonson, Molière: The Comic Contract* (1980), *Bernard Shaw: A Critical View* (1984), *Shakespeare's Tragic Imagination* (1992) and *The Politics of Irish Drama* (1999).

EMER O'KELLY is a Dubliner. She is drama critic with the *Sunday Independent*, for which she also writes literary criticism and a current affairs column. She was a member of the Arts Council of Ireland 1998–2003 and her appointment has been extended to the current Arts Council. She is a member of the Board of the Irish Museum of Modern Art and of the Ireland–Romania Cultural Foundation.

CHRISTOPHER MURRAY is Associate Professor of Drama and Theatre History in the School of English at UCD. He is the author of *Twentieth-Century Irish Drama: Mirror up to Nation* (1997) and edited *Brian Friel: Essays, Diaries, Interviews, 1964–1996*. His biography of Seán O'Casey will be published by Gill & Macmillan at the end of 2004.

LYNDA HENDERSON was until recently Lecturer in Media and Performing Arts at the University of Ulster. She was editor of the periodical *Theatre Ireland* and a member of the Performing Arts panel of the Arts Council of Northern Ireland. She has worked with Marconi and British Rail and now undertakes independent research for businesses.

JOE DOWLING is Artistic Director of the Guthrie Theater, Minneapolis. He has led the creation of the company's new three-theatre home and a national centre for arts and theatre education. He served as Artistic Director of the Peacock Theatre (1973–76) the Irish Theatre Company (1976–78), the Abbey Theatre (1978–85) and the Gaiety Theatre (1987–90). He founded the Young Abbey and the Gaiety School of Acting.

ALAN TITLEY is a scholar and writer. He is the author of novels, stories, plays and essays and writes a weekly Irish-language column on cultural and current affairs for *The Irish Times*. His plays have been produced by the Abbey, Amharclann de hÍde, RTÉ and the BBC. He is head of the Irish Department, St Patrick's College, Dublin City University.

ANTHONY ROCHE is a Senior Lecturer in the School of English at University College Dublin. He is the author of *Contemporary Irish Drama: from Beckett to McGuinness* (1994). From 1997 to 2002 he was editor of the *Irish University Review.* He is currently preparing a *Cambridge Companion to Brian Friel.*

i